sf**WP**)

www.sfwp.com

Bystanders
Stories

Tara Laskowski

Library of Congress Cataloging-in-Publication Data

Laskowski, Tara.
  [Short stories. Selections]
  Bystanders : a collection of stories / by Tara Laskowski.
     pages ; cm
  ISBN 978-1-939650-38-2 (softcover : acid-free paper)
  I. Title.
  PS3612.A857A6 2015
  813'.6—dc23
                                    2015016690

Published by SFWP
369 Montezuma Ave. #350
Santa Fe, NM 87501
(505) 428-9045
www.sfwp.com

Find the author at www.taralaskowski.com

Praise for *Bystanders*

"'Short story' and 'thriller' tend to be incompatible genres, but not in the hands of Tara Laskowski. *Bystanders* is a bold, riveting mash-up of Hitchcockian suspense and campfire-tale chills."

—Jennifer Egan, Pulitzer Prize-winning author of
A Visit from the Goon Squad

"There's still plenty left," one of the characters in "The Witness" says, referencing a cake, but the reader has been taken deep enough into the story to know that there's no way that can be true, because there's not enough of anything left for the main character. And in one story after another in this excellent collection, characters are tested when their expectations are strained and even shattered, not by the extraordinary, but more devastatingly, by the ordinary. Tara Laskowski's collection will be welcomed by readers who care about witnessing the significant rather than the spectacular."

—Gary Fincke, author and winner of the
Flannery O'Connor Prize for *Sorry I Worried You*

"Tara Laskowski's stories show off a wonderful fusion of freshness and experience. She produces time after time the energetic steps and missteps of youth and the keenly measured estimate of what it all means, that ability which for most of us comes later in life rather than earlier. Match this with her talent for employing the colloquial American tongue to bring to life time-tried and tested flaws in the human species, and you have a new writer you need to conjure with."

— Alan Cheuse, NPR *All Things Considered*

"Tara Laskowski's stories are deceptively cozy: soft suburban street lights out front, but a too-deep swimming pool out back. With a deft touch, she ravels and unravels her characters' lives seamlessly; they never know what's coming until they're in too deep, and what's scarier, the reader doesn't, either."

—Jen Michalski, author, *The Tide King* and
The Summer She Was Under Water

"In this debut that resonates, Tara Laskowski's women and men drift through an imperfect suburbia, much like the disembodied souls who haunt her characters day and night. Laskowski has a natural ability to pen the banal, juxtaposed with the horror that often lurks just outside the light that spills from our windows. She digs into the crevices and corners of everyday lives to find the grit, the dirt, the ghosts—our deepest secrets—then finds a way to turn it all into crystal clear story moments that will enlighten her readers."

—Tara L. Masih, series editor, *The Best Small Fictions*

For Mom and Dad

Table of Contents

The Witness

The boy's body hit the hood of the Toyota, slammed off the windshield, and then slid out of sight from where Marie stood. It might have been a performance, it happened so quickly, but there was no mistaking the terrible, high-whistle screeching of hot rubber on asphalt, the dull thud as the kid's body hit the street. His bike crumpled under the front wheels as though fake, made of foil. People flooded the street, retail workers, good Samaritans pulling over in their cars to help, but Marie was frozen, waiting for someone to tell her it was just a joke.

The kid hadn't even had time to scream, but a woman parked nearby wailed through her open window. At first Marie thought the woman knew the kid, her cry had been so heartbreaking. But then she began to think of it as a transfer of sound, as if the screams that the boy himself was unable to release had been conveyed through the air and into the woman, who let them out. Marie whispered, "Dear God," and pinched the inside of her wrist, something she'd done since she was a child.

The crowd went to the boy, hovering over him in a circle, everyone afraid to touch him. He was obviously dead. It was the man behind the wheel of the car Marie noticed. He couldn't have seen the boy coming with all the cars parked along the side of the street. The kid hadn't even looked, had darted out into traffic just before the light turned, and the driver, probably trying to beat the yellow light, could not have stopped in time.

When Marie walked over, the man was still sitting in his car, staring straight ahead at the mass of people. She thought he was hurt, but when she tapped on the glass with her knuckle, he looked over at her, blinked a few times, and then fumbled for the door. He must've been Marie's dad's age, in his sixties, his brown hair thinning on top, and Marie felt a stab through her heart when she met his eyes. Clear blue, the color of a glassy sky. She saw the shine of panic in them.

"Are you okay, Sir?"

He didn't answer, just struggled to get out of the car. He was tall, his legs long and thin. He placed his hands against his hips to stop them from shaking, making a deep sound in his throat. He bent over at the waist, his head resting against the trunk of his car. Then he retched, his body convulsing, and he vomited on his back tire and the street.

Marie turned away, embarrassed to witness something so private, intimate, raw. When he stood up again, wiping his mouth, she had the urge to pull him from the scene before anyone came. He turned to her, met her eyes, and said, "Thank you," his bottom lip trembling. "Thank you."

The first police car arrived, its siren wailing loudly in the cold street. The noise drowned out any words Marie might have said, and then people pushed between them, jostling her to the sidewalk, and she lost sight of him in the crowd of bystanders.

***

Bud was in the kitchen when she got home, whistling while he made a salami sandwich. She stood in the doorway watching him slap pieces of salami on the bread. She knew before he did it that he would squeeze the mustard out in a perfect spiral on the bread.

"Take a load off," Bud said without turning around.

Marie walked behind him and rested her head on his back, smelling his shampoo. This was her kitchen—the hum of the refrigerator, the broken clock above the sink, the plants that needed watering. She brushed her finger over a crack in the counter. Bud moved away from her, putting the mustard back in the refrigerator, and she almost lost her balance.

"I saw an accident," she said. "It was really bad."

He looked at her then and raised his eyebrows. "Where?" His eyes flicked over her and then at the counter, where he gestured with his hand before she could answer.

"Can you hand me those pickles?"

"Someone died. A little boy." She shuddered, still in her coat. Her voice sounded too loud and shaky.

"That's terrible." He looked concerned now, her silence making him stop. "Are you okay?"

Instead of answering, she walked into the living room. Bud followed, watching as she removed her shoes, tucked her feet into the cushions of the couch, and switched on the television. "We have to watch the news."

It was the lead story. On the television, the reporter's face took up most of the screen, ambulances and fire trucks over his shoulder. They didn't show the man Marie had helped, but the reporter said his name was Raymond Balcham.

"Raymond Balcham," Marie repeated softly, thrilled that she'd learned something more about him. He was from Old Forge, the town where she'd grown up.

"I feel bad for that man," she said, pulling her coat around her. "He looked so sad. It was awful. To hit a child. I can't imagine."

"He was probably drunk or something. I don't know how you can miss a kid on a bike, for Christ's sake," Bud said, chewing on his sandwich. He sat back on the couch, tugging on his jeans.

"He wasn't drunk, Bud. I was there with him. Why do you have to be so negative all the time?"

She switched off the television. He looked at her. "Hey, I was watching that. Don't be mean."

Marie took his crumpled napkin into the kitchen and tossed it in the trash. She brushed bread crumbs off the counter and put away the dishes on the drying rack. How many years now had she been cleaning up for Bud? Over and over again, the same routine. Make the bed in the morning, clean up after his food trail, bring his shoes upstairs to the closet. She opened the refrigerator and slammed it.

Outside, the wind whistled. It had started to snow. It was funny how her house, which minutes before had seemed quiet and safe, now seemed like a prison.

***

Marie gripped the steering wheel, afraid she was going to slide. The highway was crowded with cars going home for the day, made more complicated by the light freezing rain. After leaning on her brakes for the tenth time, Marie pulled off the highway on a stretch just before the expressway, behind a series of restaurants downtown where, as a teenager, she'd smoked cigarettes with friends.

She picked up the newspaper she'd bought at the convenience store near her office. She wanted to read about the accident alone, before she went home. In the past few days, there had been several stories on the little boy—full-page spreads in which they interviewed his family, his teachers. But what interested Marie were the reports on Balcham. It looked as though they were going to charge him for manslaughter, but his lawyers argued it was an accident. That morning Marie had looked up his name online. There were only three Balchams listed for Old Forge—Raymond F. was between Julie C. and Thomas P, and his address on Lawrence Street was only a few blocks from her parents' house.

That day there was no mention of the accident in the newspaper. Disappointed and restless, Marie got out of her car, walked to the edge of the highway. The rain had let up a little and cars passed in a blur, shaking the ground. Alongside the road, trash collected, pressed flat from the tires or caked in slush. Marie could make out a bottle of Budweiser, plastic cups, a piece of a garbage bag. She wandered slowly up the road. The mist hit her in the face, coated her hair in a fine film.

Above her, a sign for the interstate, New York City, pointed towards an exit half a mile down the road.

Heart pounding, Marie turned and faced the road. She extended her arm and thumb in the cold, watching as several cars passed, the drivers not even glancing at her. This is absurd, she thought. She felt very thin, almost transparent, could feel her breath like cold, cold peppermint running down her throat and into her belly.

A large, gray pick up truck slowed as it approached and the driver waved at her, a man around her age, his baseball cap pressed tightly atop his mop of curly hair. He grinned as he passed her, the right side of his mouth turned upward in a way that reminded her of someone, although she couldn't think who. The truck was rusting on the sides, like paint splashes around the door, and Marie could smell burning oil. The driver tapped his horn and slowed, his tires kicking up gravel as he pulled to the side of the road.

She thought about it for a moment, staring at the stopped truck, its right blinker flashing, windshield wipers flipping back and forth. The man was watching her in his rear view mirror. She could almost feel the cold vinyl passenger seat of his truck through her thin dress pants, hear an AM radio broadcasting a game. Just like that.

Then she pulled her coat around her and ran, back where she'd come from, back to her car. She was laughing, her hair curling up around her neck. She'd never tried to hitchhike before. By the time she got back inside her car, rubbing her hands in front of the vents, she was out of breath, gasping for air, her cheeks red and raw.

***

One week after the accident, her mother turned 57 and Marie and Bud drove to Old Forge after church to celebrate. Marie had made a red velvet cake, her mother's favorite, which she balanced on her lap as Bud drove. The volume of the radio was so loud they couldn't talk.

Her mother greeted her with a kiss. She smelled of roses, her makeup thick. "Happy Birthday, Rhonda," Bud said awkwardly, standing in the doorway as Marie's mother fawned over the cake.

They sat down at the table, passed around spaghetti and meatballs, salad, bread, making polite comments about the food. Marie kept looking out the window to see if it had started snowing.

"So what's new?" Marie's mom asked her, breaking the silence.

Marie wiped her mouth with her napkin. "You know that accident with the little boy last week? The one on Wyoming Avenue? I was there when it happened. The man who hit him, he lives on South Franklin Street near the bakery."

Bud looked up from his plate. "She's been talking about this all week. It really upset her."

"That's awful," her mother said. "How old was he?"

"He was around Dad's age, maybe sixty?" Marie said.

Her mother frowned. "Not that guy, the little boy!"

Her father looked up from his plate, picking up the last bits of pasta with his fingers and placing them on his fork to eat. "This is great uplifting conversation to be having on your mother's birthday."

"Well, anyway, I was questioned by the police. As a witness. It was scary." Marie pulled her hair away from her face, her cheeks hot. "I felt really awful for the man who hit that kid. He was so shaken."

No one answered. Bud took another plateful of spaghetti. Marie put her fork down and stared at the top of her husband's head.

"I saw him throw up, all over the road and his car. I was the only one who saw it."

"Marie! Not when we're eating." Her mother took a drink of her iced tea, fanned her face.

"This is how it's been all week, Rhonda," Bud said. "I told her it was unhealthy."

"Could you not talk about me like I'm not sitting right here in front of you?"

"Marie…"

"No. I don't understand why everyone is treating me like I need therapy. It was something that happened and it's been on my mind, okay? That's all." She stood up. Her mother put her hand on her arm.

"Finish dinner, Marie."

"I am finished. It's warm in here. I need to go for a walk." She got up from the table, tucking her napkin beside her plate.

"But it's freezing outside. And we're about to have cake," her mother said.

"You'll catch pneumonia," her father added, but he trailed off as she pulled her coat on.

"I'll be right back."

For a Sunday, the streets were nearly deserted. The cold had driven people inside. Marie had forgotten to bring gloves and thrust her hands deep in her pockets. She knew the neighborhood well, knew exactly where to go. Lawrence Street was on a hill, and the houses looked like they were baked into the side of it, tilted like steps. Raymond Balcham's house was halfway down, an ordinary looking white two-story with black shutters. She had half expected it to be dark, rundown, covered in gloom—a dark cloud hanging over it, she realized with a smile, but it looked like every other house on the street.

There were no signs of life except a child's red plastic snow shovel lying on the ground in the neighbor's yard. After Marie got to the end of the street, she turned back, walking up the hill, and that's when she saw the car parked in front of Raymond Balcham's house with its headlights on. It was like a sign.

She examined the car as she approached, but no one was inside. It wasn't the same car he'd been driving when he killed the little boy, but perhaps that one was still impounded for evidence. Perhaps this was a rental car, and he'd left the lights on by accident, distracted. She went to his porch, rang his doorbell, and waited. She would say what it was she hadn't been able to tell him that day on the street. She would tell him that she understood what he was going through, that she didn't think he was a bad person. That people made mistakes, had to live with the consequences of them every day.

Her head nearly touched the low, overhanging roof of his porch. The damp outdoor carpet smelled like mold, and only a small plastic table topped with a pot of dying flowers decorated the space. Something shifted inside the house, she heard a noise like someone coming, and she wanted to run.

The heavy door opened with a creak and then, as his face appeared, he let out a peal of laughter so loud that she jumped back, her hand flying to her chest. The face that had been in such shock when she first met him now grinned and his eyes sparkled. He looked at her, puzzled. "Could you hold a minute, Gracie?" he said into his phone, turning the receiver from his mouth. "Can I help you?"

Marie opened her mouth, then closed it. Balcham peered at her through the screen, his eyes dark and unreadable. They had been so clear, so blue, out on the street that day. She shifted her handbag and opened her mouth to try again.

"Miss, I'm sorry. I'm not interested in whatever it is you're trying to sell."

"I—no! I'm not selling anything. I just wanted to tell you, your car. You left the lights on."

He peered out past her, bending down to see below the awning. She pointed, her finger drooping. She knew what he was going to say before he said it. "That's not my car, ma'am. I don't know whose car that is. Thank you."

He closed the door, hard. She heard him talking loudly, retreating deeper into his house. Her anger was fierce, hot and red. She got halfway down the street before letting it out in loud, gulping sobs, crying like she hadn't in a long time, her gasps echoing in the empty street. She didn't care if anyone saw her. She kept hearing Raymond's laugh, loud and sudden, like a slap.

It grew dark as she made her way back to the house. On the kitchen table, the red velvet cake had been sliced and three dirty plates were stacked in the sink. Her father and Bud were watching football in the living room while her mother fiddled with a crossword puzzle. She looked up as Marie walked in.

"Honey? There's cake there on the table."

"I know, Mom. You guys didn't wait?" Her voice sounded on the edge of hysteria. She could see her mother examining her face, the puffiness, and knew she wouldn't ask her what was wrong.

"Well, your father—we didn't think you'd mind. There's still plenty left."

"It's ok. I'm not hungry. I want to go home, Bud."

He looked up from the television at the sound of his name and nodded. "In a minute, Marie."

She waited in the car for him, and a few minutes later Bud came out, carrying a wrapped plate of leftovers to the car. He set it at her feet in the front seat, not saying a word. It had begun to snow, wet flakes that melted as they touched the windshield.

Bud was quiet for the first half of the ride home. He kept glancing over at her. She shifted in her seat, pulling her knee to her chest.

Bud squeezed her leg, his touch tentative. "You know, I've been thinking. About us."

She closed her eyes, rested her head. The heater blew air at her face, making her skin feel raw. She wanted a cold washcloth to press under her eyes.

"This whole accident thing has really upset you, and well, I want you to know that, if you want, we could try." He broke off.

She opened her eyes. "Try?"

He glanced over at her, scratched beneath his ear. "Yeah. I mean, I know we'd said that we didn't really want kids, but if you changed your mind, you know, I don't think it's too late yet."

Her eyes widened. She laughed, a burst of noise—a cackle, really, echoing the old man, she realized. Bud tensed beside her. She caught her reflection in the rear view mirror, her cheeks red and shiny, puffed like some kind of animal. Bud was staring at her, his eyes searching hers for something, probably recognition. He must think she was crazy. She turned away.

"Oh God, look out Bud!" Her breath sucked back in a gasp. The car in front of them had stopped short at the red light, and Bud was going to slam right into the back of it. Bud reacted before Marie could brace herself. She was thrown forward as he braked, his tires squealing as he tried to swerve to the right to avoid the car. Her seatbelt cut into her chest.

They stopped inches from the car. Marie fell back against her seat. She closed her eyes. "It's over," she said.

"Yes, Marie. I'm sorry. It's ok, we're fine," Bud was saying, his hand heavy on her arm. She was thinking of the boy, the way he flew through the air like it was a circus act, so light, like he weighed only as much as a sheet of paper. She was thinking how quickly it had happened; how in only one second you could change someone's life forever. And suddenly, she knew why she sympathized with Raymond Balcham so deeply. She knew why she wanted to see him, why she kept thinking of him. It was because she was going to do the same thing he'd done. She, too, was going to kill, destroy, rip someone apart, and it was nearly impossible to avoid it.

She opened her eyes, and looked at Bud through her tears. He looked like he was ready to crumble with worry, his eyes large and focused, this man that she'd promised so much to a long time ago when they were both different people. "No, Bud. I mean it's really over," she said, and waited for the impact to register.

There's Someone Behind You

They park on the side of a dark road in front of an old railroad bridge overtaken by weeds. "This is your surprise?" Ruthie asks, her smile fading as William shuts off the car.

"Come on, it'll be fun."

Ruthie shakes her head. "You're joking. I'm not getting out of the car. Where the hell are we?"

"We're in my old neighborhood. I know exactly where we are. Come on. It's really cool."

"William, I swear to God if you're trying to scare me…" Ruthie trails off, examining the bridge. The concrete has crumbled in places, and there are hints of faded graffiti, giving it the feel of a Roman-ruin-meets-abandoned-bus-depot.

"Rootie, I used to hang out here all the time in high school. Nothing's going to happen. I promise."

She reluctantly gets out of the car, crossing her arms in front of her chest. It is mid-October but Virginia is going through a heat wave and William is wearing cargo shorts and a t-shirt that make him look very un-dentist-like. She is worried he is going through a mid-life crisis and she's part of the plan—the blonde mistress almost half his age. She would joke about it with him but she doesn't really want to know. He comes to her and drapes his arm across her shoulders. They walk along the side of the road, Ruthie's heels catching on pebbles and stones.

"Special night, my ass," she mutters.

William pinches her and she squeals, smacking him on the arm.

"I can't help it, it's cute." He sighs. "Come on, cheer up."

"You said we were going to do something fun. I didn't know 'fun' meant traipsing through the goddamn woods at night."

"I grew up ten minutes from here. I know this place with my eyes closed."

Ruthie rolls her own. They approach the bridge, a concrete arch built into a hill. The road passes through the hill under the arch, creating a narrow one-lane tunnel, and then curves sharply to the right directly after the bridge. "Jeez, that looks dangerous."

"It is." He grabs her hand and starts pulling her up the incline. The brush is overgrown but a narrow gravel pathway leads up to the railroad tracks.

"What the hell are you doing, William? Do these look like hiking shoes?"

"It's all right. I've got you. Come on. We have to get to the top."

She lets him help her, complaining the whole way. It is dark and she is too old for this shit. And yet these kind of stunts were, in part, why she had been attracted to him in the first place—he was much more fun than any other man his age. Sometimes he just went too far.

At the top of the railroad bridge, Ruthie and William stand directly over the road and look down at his lonely car. From here, the street looks even narrower. The railroad tracks are rusted, the wood between them rotting. "Is this safe?" Ruthie says, looking around at the woods. They are only a few miles from Washington, D.C., but out here it feels like the middle of nowhere. She shivers.

"I'll tell you what this is," he says, lowering his voice in a way that makes Ruthie feel like throwing him over the bridge. "It's called the Bunnyman Bridge. Years ago, a bus was transporting a bunch of inmates from an insane asylum over to Lorton Prison—"

"Fuck you, William. You said you weren't going to scare me." She punches him in the shoulder.

"Just listen, will you? Jesus, like you don't beg me to watch every scary movie ever made."

"Movies are different. You're in a theater. With seats and people around you. Not in the middle of the woods on a rotting railroad track."

"Shh." He puts his finger on her lips and in spite of herself she bites it playfully. He continues. "Anyway, the bus crashed and a bunch of the patients escaped and ran into these woods. The police caught all of them except this one guy. They started finding dead bunny bodies all around here and figured he was surviving on the meat. Then one night they finally surrounded him, and you know, he's all crazy, and just as they're about to get him, he jumps in front of an approaching train and kills himself."

Ruthie kicks him in the shoe. She is not scared, really, just a little confused by his definition of entertainment. She is still waiting for the punch line. She moves closer to him and looks up, thrilled more at the nice way his eyes shine in the moonlight than by the silly story he is telling. She likes when he teases her. She also always likes to be touching him, as if to prove to herself he's really there.

"So this place is haunted. He supposedly comes back every year and kills someone on Halloween."

"Great. Great story, thanks."

He laughs and puts his arm around her. "Rootie. Come on. Do you know what a great makeout spot this was for me as a teenager?"

"Yeah, I always get turned on by the thought of dead bunnies." She's frowning. She doesn't like to think of him making out with other women. With his wife. She wants him to herself, custom-made, one of a kind.

He snorts. "You're no fun."

She glares at him. "So, what? You were bringing me here hoping to get lucky?" She puts her arms around his neck and presses her body into his. "Don't you know there are a lot of easier ways to do that, Billy Budd?" He smells like laundry. Under his shirt, his skin is warm and damp.

He laughs. "I forgot you were easy."

Ruthie pulls away. "Whatever." She leans over the concrete ledge and looks down at the dark road below. They haven't seen even one car since arriving. "Did you bring your wife here to make out?"

William grabs her at the waist. His shoes scuff on the dirt and that is the only sound besides the rustling of the trees. "Here, Ghostie, Ghostie," he whispers into her ear. It annoys her when he chooses to ignore those kinds of questions even though she knows, they both know, she supposes, that there is no way to answer them without trouble. The black treetops bend in the wind.

William pulls away, his eyes bright from the moon. His face changes. "I think there's someone behind you, there in the woods. Watch out."

"You're a jerk." She begins the descent herself, eager to get back to the car. She can hear William behind her, and then he stops and she looks back, balancing herself. His behavior irritates her, especially in moments like these when she sees him for what he really is, a middle-aged man favoring his knee.

"Did you hear that?" His face is hard to make out and Ruthie grows angry.

"Shut up, William. Act your age for once."

"It sounded like whispering. It sounded like, 'Ruthie.'"

***

"You really are an asshole sometimes," Ruthie says back in the car where, with the radio on and the headlights beaming across the road, she feels safe.

"You loved it. You were scared." He pinches her cheek. He's got a station on that plays Barry Manilow, and she punches his radio, not really angry but still wanting to be. "Come on, I was just kidding."

"Don't you have anything good?" She turns around, rooting through his backseat, ignoring the gray basketball sweatshirt and hand-held video game on the floor. She finds a Pink Floyd CD and puts it in, settling back in her seat.

"That's Michael's music. He's got better taste than me."

Ruthie keeps her eyes closed. She doesn't like it when William brings up his son as though it is perfectly normal. But William seems to assume her silence is an invitation to talk more.

"He's working night shift for the first time tonight at the 7-Eleven and Jackie's all nervous. Every Friday night for the next month, like a damn slave, they have him working. Don't you think he's too young for that?"

"William, can we talk about something else?" Her tone is rude. Short and clipped. He calls it her 'bullet talk.'

"Sorry." He puts his hand on her knee and squeezes. "It's ok, you know. You'll get to meet him one day."

She shifts, knocking his hand off her knee. Her mood has turned black since the bridge and she hopes he blames himself. "Don't say stuff like that if you don't mean it."

He is silent. She is afraid to look at him. It is supposed to be a nice night, just the two of them. He's told his wife something. Ruthie has stopped asking what the story is. She doesn't want to know how well he lies.

"You know, I didn't tell you the whole story about that bridge," he says finally, turning down the radio. She recognizes what he is doing, trying to brush off the fight. It is an offering she can either ignore or accept.

"Yeah? What else is there?"

He grins. "Well, years later, after this Bunny Man thing had been a legend for some time, teenagers, like myself, used to go there to hang out and scare each other. In the '60s, these kids apparently went there and two of them slipped off into the woods to get it on and they never came back. They found them the next morning, gutted and hanging from the bridge."

"You're lying."

"I'm just telling you what I heard, baby. Aren't you glad I kept that one until now? If I'd told you that back there, you would've killed me."

"I believe in ghosts."

"I know you do. You were scared. I could see it."

She wrinkles her forehead. "And you liked that I was scared? Was that your purpose?" She shakes her head before he can answer and puts her hand on top of his. She loves him and it hurts, but it is even more than that, a deep, bright pang, like an itch that's so satisfying to scratch even as it stings and opens, raw. She can't shake the feeling that they are never alone, that even speeding down the dark highway right now there is someone behind them, looking over their shoulders, waiting for them to fuck up.

***

Ruthie often meets William at his office, which is only five minutes from the software company she works for in Reston and a good forty to fifty minutes from either of their houses and either of their other lives. She started going to him last year after waking up with an impacted molar. She likes his office with its little green awning out front, located in a brick office park between an insurance agency and an optometrist, the professionally stenciled "William Fairfield, D.D.S." in silver letters on the front glass door.

The receptionist in William's office looks up at Ruthie with a tired expression, her pointy nose smudged as though she'd rubbed it all over the newspaper she is reading. "I'll let him know you're here," she says, grabbing a file folder and disappearing through the door to the back offices. Ruthie wonders, as always, if the woman says the same thing to William's wife. The thought makes her blush.

In a few minutes, William pokes his head through the door and motions for Ruthie. She is excited, as always, by the way he looks dressed up. Today it is a beige Nautica dress shirt with a silver, beige, and navy blue-striped tie.

In the examining room, he closes the door behind them and kisses her, his hands spreading through her hair and massaging her scalp. "You smell good," he mumbles in her ear.

"Dr. Fairfield, I'm not sure this is professional behavior."

He pulls away, all business. "I know. I'm sorry. It's been a crazy week, and I'm leaving for that conference thing this weekend—" Ruthie pouts, her head tilted, and William grabs her bottom lip and tugs playfully, "but I wanted to see you before I left. And here you are."

They go to a small Italian deli a ten-minute drive from William's office. Whenever they meet for lunch, they choose from a variety of places around their work areas, busy restaurants where people don't pay attention to other people. Ruthie doesn't like the smaller, quieter places. They make William nervous, always glancing around.

The line is long and Ruthie sits at a corner table to save them seats. William stands with his hands in his pockets, whistling. He is a good foot taller than the rest of the people waiting in line. The man behind him taps him on the shoulder. "Bill Fairfield?" William turns around and looks, his eyes dawning recognition. She knows he hates being called "Bill."

"Paul! Hey, buddy! What's up?" William offers a strong handshake, his face breaking into a smile that makes him even more handsome. Ruthie crosses her legs, leaning over the table to watch him. "How've you been?"

They exchange pleasantries. William glances quickly over at Ruthie. The line moves ahead and the two men shuffle forward, still talking. She can tell William wants to end the conversation but doesn't know how. The other man is persistent, talkative, his hands flying everywhere. He has to look up at William to talk with him.

"So, just on a lunch break? Are you here alone? Want to sit down and catch up?" Paul glances around the deli, no doubt looking for an empty seat, and his eyes rest for a moment on Ruthie. She glances away, out the window, and hears William reply, "No, actually. I'm just picking up this order to go. It's crazy at the office today."

"Oh. Right. Well, someday we'll have to play golf again."

"Definitely," William answers.

***

Ruthie is sitting in front of her television, drinking bourbon and eating Milky Ways wrapped in orange and black paper. On the news, the anchorman reads a story about a young girl who's gone missing after a costume party at the local YMCA. She was last seen wearing a witch's hat and cape.

William is at his conference and Ruthie is waiting for him to call. She picks up the phone and tries to reach her friend Julie, who just got married, and when there is no answer, she calls two other friends. Even her mother isn't home, her upbeat voice on the answering machine making Ruthie feel even sadder. She hangs up and wanders through her apartment. She feels like everyone else is doing something, going somewhere, and she is home missing William. It makes her angry. She is sick of her place. All these things.

The news anchor comes back for a story on trick-or-treating safety. Parents are urged to make their kids wear reflectors and go in groups to familiar neighborhoods. Ruthie decides she has to go out. She does not want to be at home, waiting like an obedient little mistress, if William calls her. She wants him to wonder.

It's late, almost 11:00 p.m., and there is nowhere to go. Ruthie turns on her radio and Pink Floyd is playing "Dark Side of the Moon." She drives past the Save Mart with its blinking neon sign and thinks of William's son, Michael, working late at the 7-Eleven. She checks her watch. He will be getting off his shift in an hour, going home to his mother, sleeping in his safe bed down the hall from where his father usually slept.

Ruthie sings along loudly to Pink Floyd, happy to be on a mission. The gas pedal feels powerful against her thin ballet slippers. She is glad it is still warm, one last hurrah before the winter comes. She can drive with the windows down and feel the air rip through her hair and lift it off her shoulders. She knows the neighborhood where William lives, just a few blocks from the 7-Eleven. She's memorized his address—7890 Peace Rock Road, such a lovely, permanent-sounding address—and even drove past his house, speeding, one night coming home alone from a bar, one night after they'd kissed but before she'd slept with him, swearing to herself she wouldn't but knowing already that she would. She is already a sinner. There can be no harm in just seeing his son, no harm at all in just looking.

She pulls into the parking lot of the 7-Eleven. The windows are covered in advertising posters and look dim and greasy. Two Hispanic teenagers are standing outside smoking. They look her over as she walks past them, eyes up, then down.

A hard rock station is blaring inside and Michael is there, his back turned to her, sweeping the back counter. It is all so ordinary. She doesn't know what she was expecting. Michael turns around and glances at her, just for a second, and turns back to what he is doing. He is tall, like his father, and skinny, hair dyed black. The thick chain around his neck looks like a dog collar. Too young to be punk, Ruthie thinks. William must hate it.

She turns down the first aisle and grabs the first thing she sees, which is peanut butter, and heads to the counter. She is nervous. She pulls her top away from her skin, smoothing it down, wishing she'd worn a bra.

Michael barely glances at her as she places the peanut butter jar down on the counter. It is plastic; it doesn't make a satisfying sound. The jaunty letters in green, blue, and red seem to mock her, to make her purchase seem even more silly this late at night, like she is a pregnant lady seeking to fulfill a craving. She feels like she has somehow given herself away, though this kid would never suspect. Then in her para-noid mind flashes a thought, a picture of the future. The two of them finally meeting properly somewhere down the road—Michael stepping forward ruefully to shake her hand and it dawning on him—she was the lady buying the peanut butter that night, that hot fall night at the 7-Eleven. "Long night for you, huh?"

He grants her a quick shrug.

"Two forty-five," he says.

"Can you add a lottery ticket to that?"

He rips a ticket off the roll under the counter and hands it to her. Their eyes meet briefly; she sees a flicker of something that makes her more confident. "I'm feeling lucky tonight."

He doesn't say anything, and she laughs, a loud sound that echoes through the store. "Good luck," he says, handing her change. She uses one of the quarters to scratch off the ticket, blowing the shavings off, and then hands it to him. "Fifty bucks."

"No shit!" He grabs the ticket, his fingers brushing hers.

She pauses a moment. "Just kidding. I lost."

"Oh." He blushes.

"I'm never lucky. Are you?" She leans forward over the counter, closer to him. "I bet you're a lucky kind of guy."

In the mirror above the counter, she sees herself, aware that her top hangs low, exposing the tops of her breasts. She notices him look, quickly, and glance away. His neck is red. She laughs, remembering how his father steadied his glance at her cleavage that first date until she blushed. The boy had a lot to learn.

She straightens up and grabs her peanut butter. "Goodnight!" she says cheerfully, winking. At the door, she almost runs into a teenage girl with long dyed black hair. Her lips are a dark purple, almost black. Amateur. Ruthie watches from her car as the girl flips her hair over her shoulder and kisses Michael, her bony hips exposed above low jeans. The Hispanic kids have turned their back on Ruthie, talking into their cell phones.

***

The peanut butter is good, and as she drives through William's neighborhood Ruthie eats more and more of it with her fingers, digging out gobs of it. She wonders if William has called yet. Oh, what would he do if he knew what she was up to! And how annoyed he'd be about what the sugar was doing to her teeth!

The blocks in his neighborhood are short and littered with stop signs trying to dissuade her from continuing on. It is a rich area of town, the houses large and hung back from the streets, hidden in part by thick-branched trees. William's house is one of the smaller homes in the neighborhood, a corner house that sits diagonally across his lawn, segmenting his backyard into a triangle.

Ruthie pulls over halfway down the street and gets out of her car. The wind picks up, cooler now. Shadows lurk everywhere, dark spots where things remain hidden, undefined, and Ruthie hurries to the sidewalk where the trees shadow her.

She can see a black and white television casting a dim light on the porch, but William's wife remains hidden from view. Ruthie will have to cut across the neighbor's yard and maneuver her way through the line of trees to get a better look.

The neighbor's yard is very dark—the people are either asleep or not home—and Ruthie feels safe crossing their lawn. She can't see the ground at her feet and steps tentatively, trying to be as quiet as possible. She makes her way to the trunks of the first row of trees and looks around them, startled at how close she is now to William's back porch. From this angle she can see the TV screen—a newscaster standing in front of a storm-wrecked beach. It is still hurricane season. Ruthie feels a deep stir in her stomach, verging on fear and something else, an excitement, a secret. William would enjoy this, she thinks, remembering their jaunt to the Bunnyman Bridge. She is looking down, pressing onward without really thinking about what she is doing. The rough bark of the tree on her palms grounds her and she has the urge to hug it to feel its hardness against her body.

The light is on in an upstairs window. A woman's red scarf and hair dryer hang next to a mirror on the wall. She imagines his wife wrapping the red scarf around her delicate neck, surveying herself in the mirror, her mirror, in her house. It pushes Ruthie on. She needs to move farther down the line of trees, smack in the middle of William's backyard, where the television light will cast on his wife's face. Jackie. Whenever William says her name in passing, it hangs in the air.

She creeps along, slipping on the roots of the tree, scraping her leg on the bark. She hates the darkness; you never know who else could be there. The yard smells vaguely of dog shit—William has never said anything about a dog.

Ruthie walks into a spider web, the feathery feeling of the net across her face makes her spit, rubbing her skin and hair vigorously. She can hear the TV now. It is very low, maybe so it doesn't disturb the neighbors, and maybe so Jackie can hear her son return home safely.

"Jackie." Ruthie whispers the woman's name, imagining William saying it in the dark. It is all so perfect, the silk scarf, the screened-in porch, the sound of crickets. From behind the tree, she whispers again, this time fierce and loud.

"Jackie!"

Nothing happens.

Ruthie forces herself to move. She is one now with the darkness. It is her friend. She is not a Jackie, she is a Ruthie. She is not sure what that means, but in the spirit of things she believes it, imagining she would rather impale herself on the picket fence, trickle blood down onto the lawn, than be on the other side. At least from here she can still run.

William's backyard is narrow, and she is now only a few yards from the porch. She rounds a tree, bracing herself, and hits her shin on something hard and sharp.

The pain runs up her leg. She bites her lip to keep from crying out. She can make out what it is, the lid to an old barbecue grill balanced on a tree stump. The grill sits next to it like a silent gremlin. Ruthie smiles and pushes the lid over into the grill, startled still at the loud sound it makes as metal clangs on metal. She shrinks back behind the tree, rubbing her shin. The noise echoes through the neighborhood like a shot and stirs William's wife from her seat.

"Who's there?" Jackie's voice is loud but Ruthie can hear the fear. "Michael?"

Ruthie tastes blood. She leans hard against the tree and whispers the woman's name again. "Jackie!"

It sounds like a growl and it stirs something deep inside her, below her belly. She can sense the woman's fear pressing into the darkness and it shames Ruthie at the same time that it excites her. *Jackie, Jackie, Jackie.* Her breath comes loud and fast, and she is sure the other woman can hear her, sure that Jackie is standing behind the screen door, just a few feet away, hesitating. She won't come out into the darkness, Ruthie knows. No one ever wants to find out for sure.

The Monitor

Myra and Corey hadn't expected anyone to shell out all that dough for the video baby monitor, and they only registered for it hoping to be able to scrape together enough gift cards, coupons, and cash to buy it after the shower. But Myra was pleasantly surprised (and grateful) when her Aunt Verna mailed it to her just a few weeks before the baby was born, with a nice note that mentioned that although she never had the pleasure of becoming a mom herself, Verna thought a video monitor would come in mighty handy for new parents.

And the monitor did come in handy, very handy in fact, when Eva proved to be a colicky, fussy little thing. Although cute as a button, Eva was a handful. Thrusting and screaming and spitting up more than her body weight, it seemed. So wiggly and terrified and just plain unhappy most of the time that Myra had more than once scared herself with thoughts of throwing her baby clear across the room. And when the child did fall asleep, more often out of pure exhaustion from crying than from any of the show-and-dance rocking and cooing and shushing and swaddling that Myra did—while Corey watched helplessly from the doorway, always a whiskey in hand, his other running through his hair in that nervous way that Myra was sure would make him bald one day—Eva tossed and turned restlessly in her crib, always just one twitch away from waking again and wailing in that way that turned even the sweetest of hearts to stone.

So they used the monitor often. It came with a small handheld video screen that could be easily lifted from its charging station and carried around the house. Myra propped it on the washing machine while she did laundry in the basement, or tucked it in her sweater pocket while she vacuumed, careful to check it every few minutes to make sure everything was okay. Some days Myra would hold the monitor in her hand and collapse on the couch for a restless nap, her head whirling with all the things she should be doing, that she couldn't get done. Exhausted. Always. The schedule was relentless, murderous. Myra hated every single one of her friends who had told her how blissful motherhood was.

When Corey went back to work, Myra started sleeping in the spare bedroom so that he could get his rest. Myra was the first one to get up when the cries came, anyway. She was the first one to go to the baby, to warm up the bottle, to change her diaper. Myra's body adjusted so that every two hours or so she would wake up, startled, even if the baby wasn't crying. She would roll over, squint, examine the tiny screen for evidence that the baby was still alive. Wait for a twitch or a sigh or some sign of life before she would try to go back to bed.

Imagine her surprise when one night, half asleep, exhausted, Myra rolled over to check on the baby and it wasn't hers. The crib was a darker stain, not white. Where Eva's name was spelled in pink wood cuts above the crib there were instead three pictures of airplanes. Myra jumped up, shook the monitor. In the process, she knocked over her glass of water, spilling it all over the carpet and herself. She cursed, loudly, and from the baby's room, a muffled but distinct wail. Eva was awake, and unhappy. And yet, on the monitor, the baby was sleeping soundly.

In Eva's room, Myra leaned into the crib to soothe her sobbing child. And on the handheld monitor, nothing. Not Myra's infrared image, not her nursing nightgown bought when she was still hopeful she could swing the breastfeeding thing. Just a quiet, dark, peaceful room with a perfect sleeping child, hands sprawled above his head.

She had heard about these things, about monitor frequencies getting crossed, and it bothered her that the neighbors might be able to see her struggling with her fussy, colicky child, judging her and the weight she'd gained, pitying her for her difficult baby. She picked up Eva and moved out of the line of the camera, rocking her in the corner of the room.

The next morning she told Corey about the incident. "It's got to be the people across the street," he said. "Who else do we know around here with an infant Eva's age?"

Myra could never remember the names of the couple across the street. They'd introduced themselves several times, but she still could never keep it straight, Ted and Ally, or Ned and Eileen, or something like that. Eileen/Ally was a jogger, jogging right up to the end of her pregnancy, which pissed Myra off. Every time she and Corey would run into them outside, Corey would point at Eileen/Ally's belly and say, "Must be contagious." It was sort of funny the first time.

"Do you think they can see us?" Myra asked, wanting to close all the curtains in the house, lock the doors. She pulled her sweater tighter around her, rubbed her tired eyes. "I find that really creepy."

"Maybe not," he said. "I'll read the instruction manual tonight to see how to prevent that."

※ ※ ※

Corey didn't end up reading the instruction manual, and so when Myra woke up at 3 a.m. that night, she saw that the frequency was messed up again, and that the baby across the street was once more sleeping with his hands pressed together like an infant in a damn Anne Geddes calendar. His bedroom was bigger than Eva's, and from the angle of the monitor she could see past his crib to the door, which was open and led into a hallway and the staircase. The houses across the street were more spacious than Myra and Corey's place, and Myra found herself slightly envious of the larger nursery. She studied the room on that grainy monitor, fascinated despite herself. What were their lives like? Were they both sleeping peacefully with such a good baby? Did they have sex—a lot?

When the flash of movement came in the top corner of the monitor, Myra thought she'd just imagined it. But then she saw it again. A face, peeking into the room. It was a little boy. Like he was playing peek-a-boo, his face would appear in the doorway and then duck back fast. The baby continued to sleep.

Myra didn't remember the couple across the street having another child. In fact, she distinctly remembered a story that one of the gossipy neighbors told her one afternoon while she was out on a walk—a horrible anecdote about a late-term miscarriage, Eileen/Ally not only having to deliver the dead baby, but also deal with strangers' well-meaning comments and congratulations when afterwards she still looked pregnant. Myra remembered feeling awkward, knowing something so private about a neighbor she barely knew—it was part of the reason why she tried to avoid the woman whenever she saw her on the street. It was also (and Myra felt awful about this) part of the reason why she judged her for jogging so late into the pregnancy. Wasn't she worried about it happening again?

Myra watched the monitor closely for another few minutes, but the little boy's face did not appear again, and she convinced herself she'd just imagined it. The monitor's screen was so grainy anyway; it was easy to see something that wasn't there.

***

Corey wanted Myra to go to the doctor and get on meds for post-partum. Myra didn't want to get on meds. She didn't want to walk around like some happy zombie, unable to feel anything. It was normal, after all, to go through some depression after a baby. To feel a little hopeless. She'd read about it, talked to friends who had the same issues. Myra had cried every single day for the first four weeks, and it would've been longer than that if she hadn't felt like she needed to hide it from Corey.

All the books said this was normal. Babies so young—they don't *do* anything. They don't smile, they don't play. The first month of Eva's life was crying, pooping, eating, or some version of that cycle. Myra hadn't been ready for this kind of thing. She found herself weirdly creeped out by her child—how wrinkly she was, how delicate, how helpless, rooting around Myra's breasts in the middle of the night like a parasite, staring off into space. Sometimes the child would focus intently on a spot just behind Myra's shoulder, and it reminded Myra of the stories her mother used to tell her about feeling like the ghost of her father was in the house with them, watching, guarding.

There was only one time when Myra thought Corey might be right about the postpartum. It was one evening after a particularly hard day with Eva. The baby woke up from her morning nap and wouldn't stop crying. She cried for nearly three hours straight before passing out from exhaustion, then woke up an hour later and started crying again. Corey was late coming home from work, and in the dim light of the early evening, Myra felt like she was going to die. She had the strongest urge to hit her baby on the head until there was silence. Blissful, peaceful quiet. It scared her so badly she took Eva upstairs and put her in her crib, where she was safe, and walked out. Took a long, hot shower. When Myra got out, the baby had cried herself to sleep again. She never told Corey.

***

Myra was cleaning dishes when she saw the neighbor come outside with her baby. She wiped her hands, picked up Eva from her swing and walked outside with the pretense of getting the mail. She waved at the neighbor casually, and when she smiled back, Myra crossed the street to talk.

"Hi, I'm Myra," she said.

"Right. I'm Elly," the woman said, stretching out a free hand. "How are things going with the baby?"

"Oh, we're doing well. How about you?"

"Great. I mean, it's hard, but we're doing pretty well. Liam might be teething now, I'm not sure. You know. Always something new."

Myra nodded. "Well, that's good." She felt nervous, like she was on a first date. "I just wanted to tell you that the other night I think our video monitor signals got crossed. You have one, right? I woke up in the middle of the night and saw another baby and it scared the hell out of me, as you can imagine." Myra laughed, shifted Eva in her arms. "I wasn't sure if that was happening on your end, but I just wanted to make you aware."

"Oh wow, really?" Elly looked slightly ill at ease. "Oh, that's so weird. No, I haven't noticed that." She blinked. "How did you know it was us?"

Now Myra felt a little odd. "Oh, maybe it wasn't. I just assumed, since he's around the same age. Airplane pictures in his bedroom."

Elly laughed. "Yeah. Wow! That's so weird! I'll have to see if we can change the channel or something."

"I mean, I've read about this happening, so I guess it's not that uncommon. But I just wanted to let you know so you don't get freaked out if it happens on your end."

They chatted for a few more minutes, and then Elly said she had a doctor's appointment and they parted. "Oh," Myra said, turning back, "I just wanted to say that I'm home, you know, if you ever need anything or wanted to go for coffee or something." She blushed a little then, hoping she didn't sound too desperate. "I mean, just let me know. I know you have guests visiting now, but maybe after they leave."

Elly looked puzzled. "We don't have people visiting."

"Oh, I thought you had a little boy there." Myra fumbled with her hair.

The woman shook her head. "Nope. Just us. That's about all we can handle now. My mom was here for a few days and I basically had to kick her out. Drove me nuts." She paused, pulled out her car keys. "But yeah, that would be great. Coffee or something. Just let me know."

***

Myra saw the little boy again that night. He was standing in the doorway this time, watching the sleeping baby. He kept putting his hands together slowly, like he was clapping but not making any noise.

This time she woke up Corey, shook him, and jabbed at the monitor. "Look at this. Look. That's a little boy, right?"

Corey rubbed his eyes and pulled on his glasses with a big sigh. He sat up and took the monitor from her. Then he glared at her. "It's Eva."

Myra grabbed the monitor back from him and nearly started to cry. "Maybe the signals only cross in certain parts of the house."

Corey sighed, fell back on the bed, and pulled the covers up. "I have a 7:00 a.m. meeting, Myra. Seven a.m."

"There's a boy in that room, Corey. I'm telling you."

"So what?"

"So she told me she didn't have a little boy, that they didn't have anyone staying over."

"Maybe you heard wrong," he said, his voice muffled under the sheet.

"I didn't hear wrong, Corey," she said, her voice high and desperate. She was on the verge of tears. It was the same emotional craze she felt in those first few weeks, always on edge, tense, feeling like she was not going to make it through the next hour, the night, the days and months ahead.

"Well, Jesus, Myra, what do you think it is? Do you think they've kidnapped him and are holding him secretly? He doesn't look like he's being abused, does he? You need to go back to sleep. You don't function well without sleep."

Well, I would function a lot better if you helped out more, she wanted to say, but she held her tongue knowing that would get her nowhere. Hands shaking, she went back to the guest room and flung herself on the bed. When she looked at the monitor again, Eva was lying on her side, her arms tugged loose from her swaddle.

***

She googled "monitor signals crossing" and came up with nothing much to help. She found an article from a mother praising the new baby monitor technology that prevents that problem, and had the urge to email her. She found a lawsuit a man filed claiming his neighbor was watching his wife breastfeed their baby. She found advertisements, ratings, but nothing that told her how to fix the issue.

She just wanted things to be normal. She didn't like to feel out of place, to not be in control, to not understand. She didn't like the clutter that suddenly took over their house—swings that Eva didn't like, toys she didn't play with, burp cloths and bibs and bottles and nipples and blankets. So many blankets. Myra could not walk through a room in their house without tripping on something, stepping over something, bumping into something. That alone was enough to drive someone mad.

So the boy was just another unexplainable, irritating, and frightening piece of clutter in Myra's life. What was the issue? Was the monitor not working properly? Who was the boy? Was it another neighbor besides Elly who also happened to have airplanes in their son's room? Airplanes were a common theme, all over Baby's R Us. All the rage, really. That was an explanation, maybe, but it didn't make Myra feel much better. She was watching some other family, some unknown family around the corner or down the block. And they were probably watching her.

And yet the alternatives were even worse: Elly was lying, for one, and why would she do that? Or even worse, Myra was hallucinating the whole thing, making it up in her mind, freaking herself out, and if Corey found out, what would he do?

***

Just after Eva turned three months, Corey announced he had an out-of-town work conference he had to go to. Two nights alone with the baby—two full days and nights with no help whatsoever. "You have to tell them you can't do it," Myra told him. "You have to tell them. I'm sure they will understand."

"I can't," he said, not meeting her eyes. Myra realized how much she'd grown to hate him these days for doing this to her. For being so damn distant and not even caring about it.

"You can't? What do you mean you can't? You mean you won't," Myra said. "Is Ann Marie going, too?"

"Call your mom or someone. I'm sure you can find someone to come stay and help out."

"So she is. Well that's just great."

"It's work, Myra. Work. Our living, remember?" He sharpened the end of each word like a knife.

Right, she remembered. Back when she first found out about the baby, eager, gleeful really, to give her two weeks notice at the office. And the looks her work friends gave her, *are you sure you want to stay at home*, words she chalked up to jealousy. They were envious of her new life—no longer would she be chained to an 8:00 to 4:30 work day, a half-hour lunch break, those endless dreary meetings.

She didn't know it would be like this. Corey taking the promotion that would force him to work longer days, to supervise Ann Marie and her short skirts and chirpy laugh. Myra's days were so long, and no one to talk to but herself. *Call your mom or someone*, Corey said, but she didn't want to call anyone. She didn't want anyone else taking up her time, seeing how she wandered around the house, unsure what to do, how to be a mom.

The first night Corey was gone, Eva sensed something was different and cried for two hours before falling to sleep past 10:00 p.m. Myra didn't even bother to put on pajamas, she just tossed herself across the bed and fell asleep on top of the duvet. When she woke up, she was disoriented. It was dark. She heard a humming of some kind coming from the monitor and when she picked it up she saw those airplane pictures above the crib, that sleeping, quiet good kid that wasn't hers.

"Oh for fuck's sake," she said aloud, her own voice somehow comforting in the dark. "For fuck's sake. Aren't you ever awake? Can't you cry or something? Throw a fit? Something?"

The screen went white for a few seconds, and she heard a noise, like a laugh or a cough. Then the room again, and the little boy she'd seen before standing in the middle of the room, looking at the baby. He's going to wake him up, she thought, and Myra felt this dread, this sense of foreboding, danger. Fear. She didn't want that little boy in the room with the baby.

She wished she had the neighbors' cell phone numbers. She might've called them, warned them, no matter how stupid it sounded. "You have a little boy in your baby's room." But then again, it wasn't the neighbors across the street. It couldn't be. They didn't have another child.

The boy turned and looked up at the monitor. He smiled, cocked his head in the way that most little kids do to melt your heart. But for Myra, it sent a shiver through her core. She felt hot, scared—that raw terror like the time she left her niece Samantha browsing in a jewelry store in the mall and then couldn't find her. The boy was staring at the camera, staring at Myra, she thought, his eyes glowing green in the infrared. Then he laughed. A high giggle that seemed to echo, and came closer, lunging at the camera. Myra screamed. The monitor screen went fuzzy, and then the digital words NO SIGNAL printed in red. Through the wall, Eva's cries. The baby was fine, just startled from Myra's scream. She held her anyway, rocking her back and forth, trying to calm herself down more than the baby.

They're messing with me, she thought. She peered out the blinds in the baby's room, looking across the street at their house. It was dark, no sign of life. Their garden flag flapped in the wind.

Myra poured herself a glass of red wine and sat at the kitchen table in the dark. It was so quiet for once that she could hear the ticking of the wall clock. She drank the wine too fast. It had been so long since she'd had anything to drink. She'd wanted it, oh how she'd wanted it—read many articles online while pregnant about how a glass of wine here and there was no harm—but Corey was very adamant about it. And after the baby came, and Myra was trying breastfeeding, Corey still worried about the effects of any alcohol on Eva. Even now, he frowned on it, telling her it would just add to her depression.

But he was away. So screw him.

She poured herself another glass, slightly larger this time, and wandered into the hallway, peering through the front door's glass to the street outside. The neighbors' house was still dark. Buzzed from the wine, Myra wanted to turn on the baby monitor, even as a feeling of dread seeped through her. She wanted to know and yet didn't.

Myra carried a third glass of wine upstairs with her. She read for a while, keeping the bedroom door open so she could hear Eva if she started crying. Around 2:00 a.m. Eva did wake and Myra went into the baby's room and swaddled her arms in a blanket so she wouldn't startle herself. While waiting for her to settle, Myra peeked out at the house across the street and was surprised to find it lit up, lights on downstairs and up.

Despite herself, she went and turned on the monitor, but for once the thing was working and showed Eva's room. Myra walked around with it, feeling like some sad sort of spy, hoping for a signal to cross.

She found it, in all places, in Eva's room.

Myra sat down in the glider and watched as Elly across the street paced back and forth, trying to soothe an obviously upset son. She turned the volume down so not to wake Eva, but it was clear that the neighbor's baby was wailing and that Elly and her husband had no idea how to calm him.

Serves you right, Myra thought, and then grew ashamed of herself. Who was she to be gleeful about someone else's suffering? And yet, she couldn't help herself to feel relieved that she wasn't the only one having a tough time, that those perfect people across the street got their share of crap nights. She was beginning to think they had a bionic baby over there.

Elly paced back and forth, and Myra could see the dark circles under her eyes in the unflattering lens of the camera.

They finally got their son back to sleep. Turned off the lights. Closed the door. Myra saw all the lights in their house turn off, one by one. She imagined them settling in, pressing their faces to pillows, one ear tuned to any noise, any cry, coming from the other room. Eventually they would fall asleep, though. Myra should be sleeping, too. She knew with that same pitted dread in her stomach that Eva would be up in an hour or so, crying that pitiful lamb-like wail. Relentless.

Myra started to turn off the monitor when she saw movement in Liam's room. Something in the corner, behind the bookcase. And then, as if a spider was crawling down her back, she felt shivers. The boy. Standing up, stretching, like he'd been taking a nap back there. Or hiding.

She watched with horror. He walked over, peered down at the sleeping baby. Then up at Myra. Smiling. Waving. Then he rocked backwards, holding on to the crib railing for support, and pushed himself up. She saw him sling his body into the crib. There was a loud noise, a horrible, scary cackle, and then her monitor went blank, black and white static like an old television.

She gasped, her fingers to her throat. Shook the monitor. Turned it on and off. Out the window, she could see no lights being turned back on. No sign of life, no sign of anything at all. Oh god oh god, Myra said. Her head felt thick, foggy, from the wine and she suddenly hated herself, hated everything she did, every choice she ever made. She started crying. Should she go over there? Make sure everything is okay? What if that boy...

And then the monitor screen came back. And the baby was still in his crib, still sleeping, like he'd been when his parents had put him down, and the little airplane model was spinning steadily like it always had, round and round and round.

***

"It's not depression really," Myra was telling her doctor, fumbling with the white tissue paper she was sitting on in the exam room. "I just need something, I don't know, to calm down a little. I feel so nervous."

She was aware she was not making eye contact. She was worried about sounding crazy. She didn't want to have to go talk to anyone. It had taken all she had to call for this appointment, to come in.

Just something to take the edge off.

She hadn't had more than two hours of sleep since the wine night.

"Did you try making lists?" The doctor asked while she looked in Myra's ears. She always looked at her ears, and Myra never knew why. "Lists saved me when I first had my son. Made me feel more in control, having written out the things I wanted to accomplish."

"No, no, I haven't..."

"Try that. And don't make them too ambitious either," she said, snapping closed her folder and tapping it on the desk. "Even if there are only two things on it—just try it." She smiled, pursed her lips. "If not, come back to me and we'll talk about taking something."

***

Things I Can't Tell Corey

He works too late.

I have dreams that I break Eva's fingers trying to get her shirt on.

Eva has fallen off the bed twice when I wasn't looking.

I hate him.

I want him to show me his cell phone text messages.

The tortellini pasta dish he likes so much is not low-fat.

The red tie he bought on sale is ugly.

The Boy is going to kill the neighbor's child and I don't know what to do about it.

***

Corey was reading the newspaper when Myra came downstairs. He looked up, smiled at her. "Where's the monitor?"

"I don't use it anymore," Myra said, sitting in the chair across from him. It had taken her almost an hour to put Eva down and she was tired. She picked up the section of the paper with the crossword puzzle in it.

"Why? How are we going to know if she's awake?"

"We'll hear her," Myra said, not looking up at him.

He sighed.

"What?" she asked, annoyed.

"Nothing. It's just…well, you seem very…something."

"That's articulate of you."

"See? Like that? Are you mad about something?"

She laughed. "No, I'm super happy. I've started making lists."

***

When Myra was ten years old, a girl at school told her there were ghosts everywhere. "They watch you when you get dressed and when you pee and stuff," she said on the playground, giggling, running away to snicker with her other friends. Myra still remembered that, years later, sometimes found herself wondering as she pulled on her hosiery or yanked out a tampon—was there a crowd of ghost people laughing behind her?

The ghost boy—for that was what he was, that was what he had to be—was not a friendly one. She felt as though she had to warn Elly, but she wasn't sure how. She had started taking notes on the times she saw him and what he was doing. She still felt his presence even after she stopped using the monitor and it bothered her, woke her up at night, sweaty and disoriented. He wanted her to turn the monitor back on.

On the way back from errands one afternoon, Myra saw Elly getting out of her car and she knew it was a sign. She parked next to her and got out with purpose, pulling Eva out of her car seat and holding her tight against her chest.

"Well hello there, neighbor," Elly said, cheerful, her cheeks red from the cold. "It's a beautiful day, isn't it?"

"It is, but I hear it's supposed to get cold soon," Myra said. "Helps you get your thoughts clear, though."

"I love this kind of weather—sunny, cold, crisp. Good skiing weather."

Myra had never skied in her life, so she just smiled, tugged at her sweater. She was still wearing her maternity jeans, and so she was jealous when Elly bent over to pull her child out and Myra could see the clean waistband of Elly's tight jeans. They had nothing in common.

"How's your little one?" Elly asked.

"Oh, she's great. Cranky sometimes, but you know. There's something I wanted—"

Elly slung her purse over her shoulder and locked the car. "Oh my, I know. They are definitely a handful, aren't they? Well, nice seeing you again." She turned to go, then stopped. "Oh, hey, that monitor thing. I noticed it, too."

Myra found herself flushing. "Oh no."

"Yeah, a few times. That's really annoying, isn't it? We think we're going to probably stop using ours anyway, so your problem should go away."

"That's what I wanted to tell you. I keep seeing people—other people. An older boy really."

Elly frowned. "So it's not us? That's so weird. Because I know for sure it's Eva's room. We can see the name above the crib." Then she stopped, paused. "I'm sorry—I know it's awkward."

Myra tried to shrug. Eva was shifting, fussing. Hungry again.

"It never ends, does it?" Elly said, smiling. "Always something to do!"

"True, too much. Our house is a disaster."

"Oh, I know. Especially with people staying over, right? I mean, they try to help, but it just sometimes makes much more work." Elly paused. "Is she sleeping any better?"

"Not really," Myra said. She thought about the doctor, wondered if Elly made lists. Wondered if Elly had pills. There's a little boy in your house. A ghost boy. The words sounded ridiculous, and despite herself, Myra let out a little laugh.

Elly paused, but didn't acknowledge the laugh. "Yeah, it's tough. But at least you have help, right? I mean, with Corey working long hours and such. Having a nanny must be a huge help."

Myra felt herself getting hot. "A nanny?"

"But, hey, let's try to get that coffee sometime, yes?" Elly said, moving away. "My afternoons are usually easier than mornings."

"We don't have a nanny."

"Oh crap, there I go, sticking my foot in my trap again. Well, I was jealous that you had found someone to hire to help, especially at night like that." She laughed, then caught herself. "I mean, it's not like I was spying on you guys or anything. Jeez. Just that one night it woke me up, the other night, I guess Eva was crying, and I was confused, you know, because I thought it was Liam, and I saw her—your sister or friend or whoever—rocking her and I just was a little jealous—well, no, I guess glad for you that you were getting some rest. Ha ha."

"Rocking her?" Myra's heart started pounding. She felt for a moment like she might faint, but then the world righted itself again.

"Are you okay? I'm sorry, I didn't mean to upset you. We can get another monitor, or stop using it or whatever."

On her shoulder, Eva started crying then, kicking at her side. Trying to get away. The baby was biting her own lip, pushing, looking up across the street at their house, up toward her own bedroom window. Myra wasn't certain, but she thought she saw her baby smile.

"Myra? You okay?"

And Myra could see her then, a silhouette, just a hint of some hair and a hand raised, not in a wave, but just up, pressed against the window perhaps. "Ann Marie," she said quietly, and from a great distance she heard Elly say, "What?" But then, no, there was no one—just Corey, crossing the bay windows in the kitchen, pacing back and forth, his shoulders hunched forward, talking into his cell. Myra blinked several times, looked at Elly again. "Your baby," she said, remembering now the neighbor's story about the miscarriage, the little boy that should've been.

"He's right here," Elly said, her smile wavering, backing up a little. "Maybe you should go inside?"

Myra shook her head, reaching out her hand. There was something, she was beginning to understand, and yet still none of it made any sense. "Your baby," she said again. "The one that died."

Now Elly flinched, put a hand instinctively over Liam's head and moved back. "What? You—" she shook her head. "How do you even *know*?" she hissed.

What was it then? Their fears? Their nightmares? Eva's wails grew louder, more insistent, and she pushed herself back, nearly causing Myra to drop her. Myra steadied herself, looked into Elly's eyes, and smiled. The wind kicked up then, howling as it rushed between the houses. It had a bitterness to it, that first hint of winter. The cold had arrived, and it was settling in.

Happy and Humpy

If You're Happy and You Know It...

Her mother named her Happy, hoping it would determine her fate. Happy Prudence McDonald, and for a while there in college Happy tried to introduce herself as Pru, but Happy always stuck. Even after her sister was killed, people called her Happy. And she hardly ever smiled.

She met him at a bar. They were both at the jukebox. She was looking for Kansas songs and he needed a place to set down his beer. His name was Benedict Humphreys, but all his friends called him Humpy.

He had a fat face, the kind of face that former frat guys got from drinking too much beer, but he said someone named Happy should always have fresh flowers. She would remember that for many years, even though Humpy would never buy her flowers. Never once. Not even for their wedding, at the courthouse, with all that traffic from the interstate roaring by outside the window.

If I Told You, I'd Have to Kill You

Humpy made his living writing greeting cards, bumper stickers, and t-shirt slogans—he was always good at the trite, he joked. That glib attitude made everyone laugh. He had the obvious, self-depreciating joke that broke the ice at the party. "Guess I shouldn't have worn these leather boxers on such a hot day" or "I was really rockin' my Meatloaf CD on the way over here."

He wrote the same joke five million different ways. Ha ha, you're Old. Over the Hill. Geezer Sneezer. Feeling Forgetful? Wrinkles? Gray Hair! On dud days, he just did funny pictures of animals.

When Happy told him her name, he said, "Wow, that's sad." She said, "I've never heard that one before." He said, "What's your last name? Birthday?" She said, "What's your last name? Dipshit?" After the bar they went to McDonalds and he asked if she wanted "her meal." She took so long in the bathroom that he was sure she'd ditched him, and then she was there, standing over the small table with attached swiveling plastic seats that always reminded Humpy of grade school. She said, "Move over Humpy Dumpy, I need me a french fry fix," and he was pretty sure then that he loved her.

Is That a Burden in Your Pants, or Are You Just Happy to See Me?

When they were kids, Happy followed her sister everywhere. So when their daddy brought them to his work picnic, out in the country, out where people kept horses and painted barns and mowed fields, she followed her sister behind the picnic grounds, down a dirt path she'd found. Her sister said, you have to come see, cows, *millions* of them. It had rained the day before and their pretty dresses from Belk's were brown at the edges, their shoes ruined, but it didn't matter. Happy followed her sister's back, trailing behind even though she was one year and three months older. Followed her bouncing, dirty-brown ponytail, a little damp, to where the cows were, not a million, but maybe a dozen just beyond a silly little wire fence. Their breaths like puffs in the cool air. Come, come, her sister said, approaching the fence. We can pet them. She'd smiled, already moving, the energy in her body too much for her bones. Happy remembered her sister always in motion. And before Happy could say anything, her sister shimmied under the fence, catching her elbow on the bottom wire. A bad game of limbo, really. If it hadn't rained. If she hadn't been caught underneath, maybe just a little zap, like the animals were supposed to get if they tried to stray.

Not the smell of burning. Not out here, where the dandelions popped like smiley faces. The world ending, like that. Like the shimmer of a fake movie backdrop in the wind. Like the glare from the flash of a camera on an otherwise perfect picture. Like the beauty of poison ivy, the softness of a cat belly before its claws dig in, the swiftness of a moving current, the shine of a sharp knife. Like a poof of cow's breath in the cool air.

Home Is Where Your Beer Is

He created the house for her. It was built on a small pond just outside of town. All that wood and steel, it still amazes her to think of it. He bought her a dog, too, to have something to run around that fenced-in yard. Across the pond, you could see the movie theater, a big multiplex kind of place that looked like something out of a sci-fi movie when it was all lit up at night.

She was grateful to him. For the porch with the rocker and the deluxe toaster oven and the walk-in closets and sunken tub. He added a huge bathroom with a his-and-hers suite; a powder room, he called it. And she would've loved it, would've spent many happy hours there staring at her reflection with those lights, a line of exposed bulbs like the movie stars had in their dressing rooms, if the light switch didn't give her a mild shock every time she went to turn it on. Her mind turned on him. She began to think it was on purpose. A cruel joke.

She grew tired of dirty shoes in the middle of the hallway. Of cigarette ashes in the garden, black hairs like ants in the bathroom sink. The smell of Humpy's cologne on his sweaty clothes. She resented the April Fools' jokes every year—plastic wrap on the toilet, a fake winning lottery ticket, a stuffed rat under her pillow. When he laughed, she scowled, and then his hurt face, like a toddler. "Can't you take a joke?"

What if the Hokey Pokey IS What It's All About?

They went back once, Happy and Humpy, and trampled through the high, tick-filled grass, the path overgrown since the grove owners sold the place. The fence that killed her sister was much smaller than Happy remembered it, and the field was really just a patch of farmland for those cows, only six of them there that day. Cows are so dirty up close, their white fur matted and muddy. They make stupid noises. Their teeth all crooked. As Happy and Humpy stood there watching, one cow took a shit without warning and then stepped in it. Humpy wanted to touch her. He kept trying to hold her hand, put a heavy, lumpy palm on her back. "Jesus Christ, these mosquitoes," he said, swatting, a droplet falling from his nose.

Weather's Here, Wish You Were Hot

Six years after they got divorced, Humpy ran into Happy at the post office. At first she looked at him, then past him, not recognizing him at all, and that, more than anything else, was the lowest moment of his life. He had the urge to slap himself with stamps and mail himself away, anywhere. He had lost some weight, sure, but weren't people supposed to be able to recognize others in milliseconds simply from the way they shift in line or walk or cough? Happy was struggling with two large boxes and Humpy knew, without even seeing the address labels, that they were for her two cousins that lived in Missouri, whose birthdays were only one day apart. The tag was sticking out of the back of her t-shirt and you could see the outline of her bra across her back. Those bras, with their stiff cups like mountain ranges on the carpet. He always wanted to drink a beer out of those bras. He hated them, always in white or tan, never any lace or satin, hated them so very much and at that moment, there in the post office, he longed for them.

Then she turned again and this time when she caught his eye he saw the recognition, saw the shift in her posture and the color in her cheeks.

Her mouth opened in a surprised "O" and he could see where the lipstick had started to wear off. She smiled at him and he nodded, but they waited in electric silence until both were out of line.

"You're looking well," he said.

"You too," she said. "Lost weight?"

He nodded. He tried to come up with something funny, something stupid. Nothing. His brain was mush.

"Well, I should go," she said.

"Happy—" he said, then stopped, flustered. She waited, blinking her eyes through bangs. He shook his head. "It's just, well, your tag is out." And he reached behind and fixed it.

Families Are Like Brownies— Sweet, with a Few Nuts Here and There

She stopped going to the Sacred Heart ladies' meetings because of the vibe. She thought they all talked behind her back about how she only remarried Humpy because of the baby. Her bun in the oven, as Humpy liked to say. This may have been true, but she didn't want to feel judged in a house of worship.

Besides, after Daria, she had no time to make pierogies and go to quilt bingo. Daria gave her a sense of purpose, a nice clockworked day in which to spend her time. Humpy did his part, buying Daria ironic onesies that said things like, "Little Poo Factory" and "I'm the Reason Daddy Drinks." When Happy went back to work, Humpy got up at 3:00 a.m. to feed their daughter a bottle and learned how to install the monitor, but he left everything else up to Happy and she liked it that way.

They were probably too old to have a baby. Over the hill. It inspired Humpy so much he started a new line—Geezer Parents—and that turned into gag gifts for baby showers, things like diapers with large print and arrows, burp cloths with pockets for your dentures, and baby rattle pill containers. Humpy sold the whole line to a major party store chain and quit his job to become a stay-at-home dad.

Sometimes at night after the baby went to bed, Happy and Humpy would sit on the front porch together sipping iced tea they'd spiked with vodka. It was never quite the perfect night—always a little too cold or too warm—but it wasn't so much to complain about. Happy would look out at the pond, at that brightly lit movie theater across the way, and start to feel restless. She would say something like, "If only I'd never met you, I could've been a star. Could've been in those movies, famous and glamorous, you know." And Humpy would sigh, a sound that picked off a piece of her soul like a chisel to ice.

"I know," he'd say. "You could've been something."

And then she would laugh, too hard, and poke him in the chest. "I'm just kidding, you dummy. Can't you take a joke?"

The Cat-Sitter

It was going to rain at any moment. Sullivan had risked getting caught in the downpour and instead of taking the subway had chosen to walk so he could stop at his girlfriend's favorite florist on his way to see her. He didn't mind walking, and he didn't mind the rain, really. It had been ten years since he'd moved to the city, and it still didn't get old to wander around, admiring all the massive buildings and important people surrounding him.

He and Alicia hadn't been dating for long, and the thought of seeing her still excited him. Sullivan liked her apartment building, too. He had once watched someone's cat in the same building where Alicia lived, only on a different floor. Every time he visited, he thought about himself, ten years ago, doing all sorts of odd jobs and wondering if he was going to make it. It gave him a sense of accomplishment to dwell on this, to think about how far he'd come since then, going from scooping out litter boxes to managing the front desk at one of the premier hotels in town. He liked walking so he had time to think about all of this.

As Sullivan approached Alicia's block, a little bunch of Gerbera daisies in hand, a high wind kicked up, skittering newspapers and paper cups across the sidewalk. He held the flowers close to his chest. Alicia had told him once that she never bought flowers for herself even though she loved them. "Flowers are like jewelry. You should know what you like, but let someone else buy it for you." A line of children in bathing suits filed out of the gate surrounding a city park, colorful beach towels around their bodies, as an adult urged them forward. "I said the pool's closed, hurry before it starts to pour." The air felt heavy, unbreathable, but it made Sullivan strangely happy. He felt the potential in it, the feeling that something important was about to happen. As he rounded the corner, a few fat drops landed on his shoulders and his cheeks, and then just as he stepped under the awning of Alicia's apartment building, the storm clattered down, soaking the hot sidewalks in steam, and Sullivan stepped into the cool air conditioning of the building, picking up his pace now that he was so close to seeing her.

***

Alicia's apartment was small but tidy. She had an abundance of mismatched furniture. She was fond of collecting things—an orange velvet couch from her grandmother, a rocking chair from the thrift store, a set of ceramic figurines posed on top of a bookcase, and a La-Z-Boy recliner that her dad had bought her when she graduated from college. She collected friends, too, and invited them over for dinner parties like she was a curator selecting from her finest and most eclectic paintings. Sullivan had only been included in a few of those meals so far and he'd felt a bit lost at sea trying to keep up with the conversation, which included much ado about the latest plays and movies (many of Alicia's friends were actors or artists, like herself, who were trying to make it big in one way or another). Her friends had been kind, but distant, as though Sullivan was the latest of Alicia's oddities—one of the figurines found dusty on the back shelf of a thrift store. He was always mildly surprised each time she called him to go out again.

"Which shoes should I wear?" Alicia paced around in her bare feet, holding two shoes—one a deep blue stiletto and the other a zebra print heel with a pink bow on the toe. She did not take the flowers, but she did smile at them.

It was her hair that Sullivan admired, always different, always changing.

Today it was piled on top of her head in a nest of tiny tiny braids. Last time he'd seen her, she'd had a sleek bob that accented her long thin neck.

"Whichever ones are sturdier," he said, smiling, an in-joke between them, but if she got it, she didn't react. She disappeared into her bedroom and he looked around for somewhere to put the flowers. It was how he'd met Alicia—imagine his luck!—one of her famously high-heeled shoes had snapped off in a grating outside his hotel just as she was about to meet a friend for lunch. Part of his front desk duties was to make sure all guests and visitors of the hotel were comfortable, and they actually had several pairs of women's shoes in the back room for these types of emergencies (many of them were unclaimed shoes left in the rooms). "Where were you going again that day?" he called to her, turning, and was startled to see her standing right in front of him again, a few inches taller with the deep blue shoes. He lowered his voice, smiling. "That day, when your shoe broke? Who were you meeting again?"

"Oh god, Sully, I don't remember. Probably someone for a part or something."

On the dining room table was a vase filled with fresh lilies. Sullivan stared at them, started to make a joke about another man but stopped himself. He was too embarrassed, or didn't want to know.

"Those were like five hundred dollar shoes. I need a starring role in Broadway to ever see something like that again." She sank down next to him and kissed his neck. "Or a super nice hotel manager to buy me some for my birthday."

He didn't even know when her birthday was. He didn't ask. She took the flowers from him and buried her nose in a pink one. "They are so pretty I could eat them."

***

That night when he was rinsing dishes in his sink, Sullivan thought again of the cat-sitting job. It was the crust from the chicken potpie his roommate had left on the counter. The crumbs, moistened under the water from the faucet, looked to Sullivan like wet cat food and he remembered how much he'd hated the smell. He remembered thinking he would love to have a cat if not for the food. Sullivan enjoyed other people's animals okay, but he was always relieved to go home to his own apartment with only a houseplant to worry about.

He tried to picture that client's apartment. He'd only gone there a handful of times, and he remembered the cat was sick. He'd had to inject some kind of medication in his food and mix it all up. He remembered the way the cat had jumped up on the kitchen counter, mewing desperately, pleading, rubbing up against Sullivan's arm. That place had been a little depressing, then, and overly warm.

It hadn't even been a job that Sullivan had signed up for. The job had been passed on to him when another cat-sitter had unexpectedly left town. He had met her at a coffee shop, and she had given him the key and the instructions, which was a bit off protocol for the business. Usually all keys had to be kept at the central office and signed out by each sitter when they got the new job, but because that didn't happen Sullivan had simply kept the key.

Just because he was standing right there next to the junk drawer, Sullivan rummaged through it. He was not really expecting to find it, but things did have a way of just sticking around. And there it was, in the back, under a pile of rubber bands. A heavy key. Gold. Otherwise, nothing special. He even remembered the apartment number because it was the same as the house he'd grown up in: 814.

**

The next time he went to visit Alicia, he took the key with him. Sullivan had not really planned to do anything with it, but he was a few minutes early when he got into the elevator and suddenly felt brave enough to push the button for the eighth floor. He waited nervously, a knot budding in his stomach, as the elevator slowly, so slowly, creaked upward.

What were the chances that man still lived there? Sullivan was not a thief. He could not even help himself to the bowl of mints they kept on the front desk for their customers, even though Frida the overnight housekeeper tossed handfuls of them in her apron any chance she got. He was just going to walk past the place, see the door number, make sure that he was remembering correctly.

Sullivan stood in front of apartment 814, feeling the blood thudding in his neck. Would it still fit? After all these years, surely not. The key slid in like it was slick with oil, turned soundlessly, and when Sullivan turned the knob the door swung inside like it was welcoming him in.

What am I doing? Sullivan wondered as he stepped inside. He hadn't even thought that someone might *be* here, that at any moment he could be shot by a pistol or attacked by a guard dog. But it was the middle of the day in the middle of the week, and it was clear almost immediately that no one was inside the place. Sullivan felt an overwhelming sense of anxiety stepping into the apartment. It was the smell, a rather stuffy, yet not unpleasant, odor of cleaner and air freshener—and it immediately put Sullivan back to that time ten years ago when he fell asleep with knots in his stomach, worrying about his next month's rent payment. And the apartment itself seemed familiar, like the furniture hadn't changed in ten years. It was a nicely decorated place. The furniture looked heavy and dense and most definitely not from Ikea like all of Sullivan's bookshelves and coffee tables.

I'm not really doing this, I'm not really here. That feeling of invisibility—a ghost slipping into someone else's life, for just a moment. He'd always liked that and been frightened by it when he had done all those pet-sitting jobs that summer. He enjoyed not having to see anyone, to talk to anyone—that endless pratter at the front desk always got to him—but he also sometimes felt like he could just slip away, just disappear, and no one would ever notice.

"Mew." The cat voice, so tiny and fragile. The kitten rubbed its entire body around Sullivan's legs, figure-eighting around them. There, then. The old cat must've passed on, Sullivan thought. He reached down and ran his fingers through the kitten's fur. Such a fragile thing. So trusting.

Sullivan walked cautiously around the perimeter of the rooms, checking in each open door as though he might see a younger version of himself around a corner. It was eerily quiet, only the hum of the refrigerator. A bill tacked to the refrigerator revealed the man's name was Bernie Halifax. Sullivan was careful not to touch anything. He was rehearsing a story in his head—"I'm the cat-sitter?" he would say if someone walked in right then. "They called me and said you needed help this week?" He would hold out the key, say he got it from the company. Blame them—how could they possibly have gotten something like that mixed up?

The walls in the bedroom were painted in fashionable hues—light grays, mauves, and green—and there was real artwork hung on every wall. The bed was made, closet doors were shut, and the only sign of anything out of place was the remote control tossed in the center of the bed and a pair of slippers kicked off in front of the closet door.

He felt this tremendous sense of urgency—that he needed to get out of there. And yet, he'd come this far. He just wanted to see. See what? It was like he was two people—the one who clearly understood that his actions were not normal or sane, and the person who was walking up to the framed photos on the coffee table, picking them up.

The cleaning women at the hotel always told stories about the things they saw in the rooms. Remote controls dripping in some unidentified substances; kinky sex toys left on the bed; toilets unflushed. One time Frida opened a door to a group of fluttering parrots swirling around the ceiling, one of them greeting her with a "Hello, my love."

Bernie liked photos. Every table was covered in rows of framed photographs. Sullivan looked at them. Many people smiling. Groups of people on beaches, boats, in front of trees and houses. In Disney World. In Paris. Cats lounging, sleeping, being held by people.

"Hello, Bernie," he said quietly. "What have you been up to these last ten years?" Behind him, the cat leapt from its perch on the counter and darted into the next room.

***

He told Alicia about it in bed. They had just had sex, and Sullivan always felt more confessional when he was naked and his heartbeat was returning to normal. Alicia flipped over and propped up her head, eyes gleaming. "Really? Sully, that's so naughty!" She put her chin on his shoulder. "You have to take me."

"I don't think so, Alicia. I shouldn't have even done it. It was stupid."

"Are you kidding? That's brilliant. It's like he will never even know. Like you're a ghost." She squeezed the skin under his nipple. "You have to take me. Like, now. I love looking at other people's houses."

"I think he's gay," Sullivan mused, staring up at the ceiling.

"Gay? What makes you think that?"

"The pictures on the table. There are lots of him with another guy, though I guess it could be his brother or something. He's lived there a long time. Ten years. And none of the decorations have really changed. Don't you think that's weird? Nothing? After ten years. I think of how much has changed with me in the last ten years." He put two fingers to his lips, smoking an imaginary cigarette.

"Let's go now! Before he gets home, Sully. Please?" She rolled off the edge of the bed and tossed his pants at him.

He knocked them away, pulled the sheet up over his head, but Alicia was on top of him. She held his t-shirt up to his face. Sullivan bit his lip. She smiled at him until he couldn't help but smile back.

***

Alicia pushed past him into the apartment, slinking forward, rubbing her hands on everything. She had dressed for the part, donning a black wrap dress and covering her hair with a black silk scarf. She kicked her black stilettos off and wiggled her brown toes in the carpet. She touched the photos, made an 'mmm' sound. Approached the white sofa by the window and leaned over it. "What a view," she whispered. "This is what I need. He's above the bank building." It was true. The eighth floor had a much better view of the city than the fourth.

Sullivan stood near the door, like he had something on his shoes that he didn't want to track into the room. The DNA Alicia was getting everywhere, he thought. *I'm not really doing this, I'm not really here.* She came over to him and reached inside his pocket. Tugged out his clunky key chain. "What are you doing?" he asked, but she was already back at the white leather couch. She twisted out the Swiss army knife, rubbed her finger lightly across it. "No seriously, what are you doing?" Sullivan walked toward her, grabbed her wrist, but she twisted away from him.

"Hold on hold on hold on," she said impatiently. She bent over the couch again, farther, her ass in the air. Sullivan leaned over her to see. Alicia held the knife at the back of the couch, toward the bottom, and made a tiny slit in it near the corner. "There we go."

"What the hell? Are you insane?"

She sat up, slumping next to him on the couch, and closed the knife. She smiled. "There. Just a little cut. He'll never even notice it, ever. But we'll know it's there."

"We have to go." Sullivan pushed himself up, but Alicia tugged at his shirt.

"Wait. Just a minute." She stretched her arms above her head. Yawned. "We deserve this, Sully, don't we?" Even her voice sounded different, thicker, some unidentified fake accent, like she was auditioning for one of her roles.

"Deserve what exactly?" He stood above her, adjusted a pillow on the couch.

"This. This moment." She stood up and kissed him. Wrapped her arms around his waist. Squeezed his ass. She was soft and tiny and molded to him like his foam mattress. "Don't you think so?" she whispered in his ear. He was starting to worry about trusting her with this. But despite all that, his penis was beginning to get hard as she rubbed all over him.

"Alicia—we need—"

She was breathing in his ear. "I want you to do me on the couch, while I look out at the city, Sully." She pulled away and fell on the couch again, leaning over it, her cute ass wiggling in the air. "Come *on*, Sully. Before he comes *home*."

It was not the best sex, mostly because Sullivan was waiting to hear the key turn in the lock, be caught with his pants down in someone else's apartment. In the middle of it all, the cat jumped on the couch and sat itself down on the back next to Alicia's head, just watching Sullivan with its dull green eyes. "I can't do this with that fucking cat there," he said. They both tried to shoo it, but it just persisted.

"Just close your eyes, Sully. Pretend it's not there."

Sullivan came quickly, and was relieved when it was over. Alicia collapsed, letting out a loud hiss like a teapot. He pulled her off the couch onto the floor. "We can't get anything *on* it," he said in horror, and she giggled.

"You are so funny."

She wanted to linger and he had to keep nudging her like he would a toddler. "Get dressed. Let's go." Straightening up the pillows. "How did he have them?" Putting on his shoes. "It's already after 4:00." He finally got her out the door and locked it behind him, the cat still sitting there on the back of the couch, tail twitching, eyes squinting as if to say, *I'm telling on you.*

"God, that was *amazing*," Alicia shouted as they got on the elevator. Her scarf had come undone and she just draped it around her shoulders, rolling her head along the back wall. The accent had come unraveled, too. "Simply amazing. I've never—" she started, but didn't finish.

∗∗∗

Sullivan worked the whole weekend and went drinking after his shift with some of the other guys who worked at the hotel. He gave Alicia a call Monday afternoon, and by then everything that happened in the other apartment seemed like a distant memory, detached from him. Something to tell his buddies about years from now. He decided he wasn't even going to mention it when he talked to her.

"Would you like to go to a matinee or something?" he asked once they got the pleasantries out of the way.

"I think you should come over here," she purred. She sounded groggy, like she'd not yet gotten out of bed. Sullivan wondered what he might find if he ever came over to Alicia's place when she wasn't expecting him.

He knew he should probably be pleased that she wanted sex all the time, but he couldn't help but feel irritated when that's all she talked about. "I was thinking we should go do something. It's such a nice day."

"It is a nice day. But why don't you come here first and then we can figure it out?"

When he got there, she was indeed still in her robe, cupping a mug of coffee in her hands, her hair tousled in a sexy way. She grabbed his crotch and smiled. "I've missed you."

"Alicia—"

"All weekend, no Sully." She pulled close to him, kissed him. "Did you bring the key?"

"The key?" He stalled, feeling prickles of anger in his shoulders.

"I think I may have lost my earring up there. I need to go look for it. It's evidence you know."

"Your earring? What do you mean you lost your earring?"

"You know, I think maybe, when you were…" She moved her hips back and forth and laughed. "You're so aggressive."

He paced back and forth. Was she lying to him? If the earring was there somewhere, though…He looked at her. She was smiling, biting her lip. She'd gotten to him, he realized. He remembered a story a friend of hers had told at the dinner party, some long story, interrupted by laughter, about how Alicia had once broken up with a guy by telling him she was on the run from cops because of a bank robbery. Even then, he'd stuck around for a while until one evening they were walking through a park and police sirens had come wailing down the street. "The poor chap had turned so pale you could almost see through him," this friend said, his voice choked from laughter. "Oh, Alicia dear, you really can tell some whoppers."

"I'm not going back up there again," Sullivan said. "We'll get caught and go to jail. Do you get that? It's breaking and entering. It's not a game." He wanted to tell her about the woman they'd just fired at the hotel for stealing. She'd been caught taking socks from guests' rooms. Expensive panty hose and knee-highs, a whole collection of them in her locker. But he was afraid to give her any more ideas, so he just glared at her.

"We'll just go look for the earring. That's all," she said, pouting.

"Why? Why do you want to go back there so badly?"

"I seriously lost it, Sully. It's one of my favorites. I've torn up the place here looking for it, and it's all I could think that maybe it's behind the couch up there or something."

"Fine. We'll go. But no funny stuff."

She laughed. "Funny stuff. You're so cute. Didn't you like it?"

"No, I didn't. And I'm considering us lucky we haven't been arrested yet."

"Oh, poo poo. Just one more time, Sullivan. I promise."

"No cutting things. No sex. No touching anything. Just look for the earring and go."

She held up her fingers. "Scout's honor."

***

It was Alicia that found out Bernie's schedule. She dropped it on Sullivan one evening. "Bernie works at some financial place or something—he usually gets home around 6, just after St. Mary's rings the 6 o'clock bell."

"And how do you know that?"

"Our doorman Dennis."

"You *asked* him?"

"Calm down, calm down. It was all very innocent. I told him I'd seen Bernie drop some cash as he was leaving the elevator, but I couldn't get to him in time to return it. I asked Dennis when he usually gets home so I could give it back. I ended up giving Dennis $20 to give to the guy, so you owe me." Alicia punched Sullivan in the shoulder. "But now we know he's not going to walk in on us...you know." She made a circle with her thumb and index finger and put her other index finger inside.

***

They went half a dozen times. It got to the point where Alicia wouldn't see Sullivan anywhere else. Each time she did her hair differently, played a new role like she was auditioning for something. One day a slick bob, silk suit. The next an afro and floral maxi dress that grazed the floor as she walked. She was a little girl in pigtails, a punk rocker, a country western gal with red boots.

Sullivan couldn't keep track of who she was anymore. The apartment was the only place he could really see her close up, study her, but even then it was not really her. But even the apartment seemed surreal, just a space between spaces, somewhere neither of them belonged.

Perhaps everything about Alicia was secret, an act, a put-on. On the streets sometime, he would see a woman walking with another man and wonder, for a brief moment, if that was Alicia. Most of the time she would turn and he would see the woman's nose was slightly upturned, or her cheekbones too high, but every once in a while he wouldn't be able to find the differences before she disappeared.

***

Each time, he said it was the last time they would have sex there, but after several times of going and not getting caught, it began to feel less dangerous, boring even. When they were done, she just liked to slump over the couch and look out at the view. "You know there are a million legal places in this city that have better views than this," Sullivan said.

They felt like they were getting to know Bernie. He had a good cable plan, belonged to a book club, donated money to the University of Virginia, and voted Democrat. Bernie liked almond milk and Cheetos, preferred Puffs to Kleenex, and had an affection for the Miami Dolphins.

One time they played "husband and wife"—Alicia's idea, setting the table and pretending to cook dinner in the middle of the afternoon. Sullivan figured Alicia would tire of the game soon, though in reality he suspected she would tire of Sullivan first. The entire apartment was just a set, just a bunch of props for her to tinker with.

Alicia opened Bernie's closet, ran her fingers along his clothes. "He likes blue," she said. She tried on his bowler hat and posed in front of the full-length mirror on the wall. "I think it suits me."

Sullivan stopped following her around and instead fed the cat. He found the treats in the cabinet above the microwave and sat on the kitchen floor feeding her one treat at a time. "What is your name?" he asked her. "You are a pretty cat." She always came back for more. "I am going to name you Juniper."

"Sullivan, come here," Alicia called from the bedroom. "I can rehearse my lines for the audition," she said when he entered. She was rummaging through her purse. "There. Lay in the bed." She pulled out some papers. "Go ahead. The bed."

Sullivan sat cautiously on the edge of the bed.

"In it, Sully."

"I'm not getting in the guy's bed, Alicia. That's creepy."

"Fine, whatever. You're supposed to be under the covers."

"Pretend."

She glared. "At least lie down, would you? It's important for me to get into the part."

He lowered his head onto the pillow, making sure to keep his shoes off the bed. It was too intimate for his comfort, lying on someone else's pillow, looking at someone else's ceiling. He knew they'd already crossed so many lines, but this one, this one, wigged him out.

From the doorway, Alicia started to read. "I've come to tell you something, Raymond."

"I want a cooler name than Raymond. Fabio. Or Dylan."

"Jesus Christ, Sullivan. Can you please just humor me?" He heard her flip some pages. "Now, you're supposed to say, 'I don't think I need to hear it, Marissa.' But don't worry, we'll just skip over that. Now, here's where I get into the monologue." Alicia cleared her throat and then her voice got lower, like she was trying to be someone who was trying to be serious. "It was hard enough back when we were all at Still Water, when we were all just kids, messing around…"

Sullivan drifted. He noticed little indentations on the ceiling, little pockmarks here and there, and wished he could float up and push on them, see if they would give way. He wondered if Bernie ever looked up at them and felt the same urge.

Alicia reached a part in her monologue where she was supposed to cry, and he realized as he listened to her gasp and hiccup that she probably was not a very good actress. That that's why she never really got any good parts anywhere. Like the guys at the hotel always talking about how they were going to be promoted and transferred to one of the hotel chain's other locations—somewhere warm and sexy like L.A. Everyone always waiting to be discovered.

Sullivan scratched an itch below his elbow and felt something wet. He looked and saw a small cut. Just a tiny scratch, maybe from the cat, maybe from a quick slice of a Swiss Army knife. Alicia had stopped her reading and was puzzling over the page. He waited for her to look at him and smile. The air conditioner in the unit kicked on, making everything cold, and Sullivan got up to go rinse off the blood before it stained something.

***

A few days later, Sullivan and Alicia were coming back from lunch—a rare date out—when Alicia stopped at the entrance to the apartment building. "Oh my god, that's him isn't it?" Sullivan looked over at the man who was walking across the lobby to the elevators. He recognized the sloping nose, the receding hairline. Alicia grabbed his hand. "What's he doing here so early? Come on."

"Wait," he said, but she dragged him across the lobby, her nails digging into his wrists. They stopped behind Bernie and waited for the elevator.

"I love your watch," Alicia said, and Bernie turned and looked at her. His nose was red and flaky, and he clutched a wad of tissues.

"Oh, thanks," he said in a warbled voice that threw him into a fit of rasping coughs. Sullivan stepped back, but Alicia leaned into him, already becoming someone else, already the voice slightly higher, slightly more girlish. Her flirting voice.

"It's a Swatch, right? One of those old school ones. I used to collect them when I was a kid. I had like ten different ones, and this little box to keep them in."

He nodded, dabbing at a watery eye. "Yeah, I had a lot, too. Got this one on eBay."

"Memories," she chirped, and Sullivan nudged her. She ignored him. "So you live here, too?"

The elevator doors opened and they all stepped inside. Sullivan took the back corner and pressed his entire body against it. Alicia slithered in front of him and pushed the button for the eighth floor. Both she and Sullivan reached out their hands at the same time to correct the mistake, and Alicia laughed loudly, nervously. "Oh, silly me, I keep forgetting what floor I live on." She hit the button for the fourth floor. "I used to live on the eighth floor in my other place," she said, "and I keep doing that all the time."

Bernie smiled. "Well, it's okay. Turns out I live on the eighth floor."

"Oh!" Alicia laughed again. Sullivan scowled, his face burning red. "That's so funny! Ha ha. What are the chances?" She looked up at Sullivan, and he shrugged dramatically.

"What are the chances?"

The elevator took its time getting to the fourth floor, creaking, groaning. Alicia hummed, tapping one of her ballet slippers. Sullivan was certain that police officers would be there to greet them when the doors opened—if not now, then soon.

"I've lived here for twelve years now, and the elevators have always been this slow," rasped Bernie, rubbing at his nose with the tissues. "I sometimes think about all my life that was wasted waiting for this thing to crank itself up to eight floors."

"Well, have a lovely day," Alicia said as they exited. "Take care of that cold." She just barely waited until the doors closed before turning to Sullivan and collapsing in his chest. "Oh my god, that was awful."

"I know," Sullivan said, surprised. "I told you this was wrong of us."

She raised her head and looked up at him, grabbing the front of his polo shirt. "Sullivan, no, do you not realize what this means? Bernie's sick! He'll probably be staying home the rest of this week." She stood upright and found the keys to her apartment.

"The good news is you can bring him chicken soup and he won't even have to get out of bed."

"Oh, hilarious." She opened her door and took off her raincoat. "I just don't know what we'll do all week. We'll be so bored."

"We could try legal activity. More lunches like today? That was nice, wasn't it? Or, I don't know. Go to a movie? Dinner? Order in and play a game?" He watched her retreat into the kitchen, waving her hand in dismissal.

"And how will we know when he's better? Back to work? How will we know when it's safe to go back?" When he didn't answer, she came back with two glasses of wine and handed him one. "These are all serious questions."

"I think maybe we're done," he said.

Alicia's eyebrow rose. "Done? Don't be silly, Sullivan."

***

On the day that Sullivan really decided enough was enough, he walked along the water, the heavy gold key in his pocket. He used to jog along the river when he'd first moved there, thought it might be a good place to meet people. Now he walked. Bikers and joggers passed him. Boats out in the water puttered along. He was waiting for a chance to throw the key in the water. He wanted it to be a grand gesture, but he was afraid if someone saw him he could get in trouble for littering. That was the problem with Sullivan—he was always looking to do something solid, something real, but was afraid of the consequences. So he never did much of anything.

He had an eerie feeling then that nothing had changed since he first moved there. That time hadn't really passed. He was still the same Sullivan hanging on by his teeth, living paycheck to paycheck. Ten years and he had no real friends to turn to, to talk about his relationship, to figure out what he was doing wrong. He played an occasional Xbox game with his roommate, but he had a regular day shift IT job and they hardly ever saw each other. The guys at the hotel—kids really—were still into hooking up with as many chicks as possible.

Sullivan stopped suddenly and threw himself purposefully into an oncoming jogger's path. "Watch it, shithead," the guy huffed as he passed, and Sullivan was satisfied that even if not really seen, at least he still existed.

He pulled the key from his pocket and looked at it. Just an ordinary key. Nothing special. A key that among other keys would just blend in, get lost. He thought of all the hotel keys hanging in the special box behind the front desk—for they were still that type of establishment, one that used real keys—and the story of a disgruntled former bellhop who'd removed all the tags and swapped them around during his last shift. It had taken days to sort it all out.

Just throw it, Sullivan thought then, willing himself. But he couldn't. He put it back in his pocket and walked off.

***

The next morning first thing, Sullivan went to Bernie's by himself. He fed Juniper almost an entire bag of treats that he bought at the 7-Eleven. The cat had started waiting at the door for him, scratching with her paws as he approached, almost like she could smell him. "Goodbye, kitty," he told her, scratching behind her ears. The cat slinked away, unimpressed.

Sullivan opened Bernie's closet door and flicked through the suits. Sullivan didn't own an expensive suit, but he knew one when he saw it and there were many of them. He reached back to the edge of the closet and pulled out a dark blue suit that still had dry cleaning tags on it. The receipt stapled to the hanger had a date from two years ago.

The sleeves were a little long. The pants were a little snug, but the right length. Sullivan chose a crisp white shirt from the end of the rack. He did not put on a tie. He fingered the socks in the dresser, thought of the cleaning woman's locker, and left them there. Bernie's shoe size was one too small, but Sullivan was wearing his black dress shoes from work. He folded his own clothes in a shopping bag.

He locked the door behind him. He held the key up for a moment, as if making sure it was the right one, and then pushed it under Bernie's front door, giving it one final shove so it would move out of his reach. He got down on his belly and peered through the crack, saw the key a few feet inside, saw Juniper's little paws scamper over, her nose sniff the key. He smiled, then got up, straightened out his suit, and headed for the elevator.

***

"I gave it back," he said. "The key."

He was talking through Alicia's door. He knew she didn't like it when he just showed up without telling her, but he had to do it now or he was afraid he never would. There was silence on the other side, and he wasn't sure she was going to let him in. Then he heard the metal slide and the doorknob turn and there she was. That brown hair, wavy this time, all around her shoulder with a thin, gold, braided headband holding her bangs away from her face. Full pink lips slightly open, wide eyes staring at him.

"Why?"

He wanted to kiss her, but he walked past her. The air felt thick, and he sensed he was interrupting something. She closed the door slowly, still staring at him. "Why? You know why. It just—it wasn't right."

She shrugged, picked up the remote, and shut off the TV. "I figured you would."

"Are you upset?" He followed her into the bedroom. The bed was unmade, sheets twisted and hanging off the bed. He had a feeling he'd just missed something or someone.

Alicia picked up two bottles of nail polish off the dresser. "What do you think—the pink or the orange?"

"It just wasn't right. We just couldn't keep violating that guy's privacy like that, don't you agree?"

She smiled. "Totally. The orange." She put the other bottle down and wiggled to the middle of the bed to start painting her nails. "I agree, Sully. We can't keep being places where people don't know we are."

Did he hear someone clear his throat? He had an urge to look under the bed—knew suddenly that they were not alone. Someone else was there. In the closet? Under the bed? Alicia calmly painted her nails, like she was waiting.

"Well, okay. I'm glad we agree." He paused. The suit was bunching and pressing in places it shouldn't, and he was growing increasingly uncomfortable. "So, would you like to get dinner?"

"I've got plans tonight, Sully."

"Tomorrow then?"

She looked up at him and shook her head slightly. He wanted her to say something then, something about how he looked. Or kiss him. He really wanted her to kiss him. She raised a finger up to her lips, and broke into a triumphant grin. "Busy then, too. I guess you'll have to wait until next week."

He had this funny idea then that Bernie himself was under the bed and that this whole scenario, the whole crazy deal, had been part of some bigger plot, that Bernie and Alicia had been pulling one over on him this whole time. Silly stupid Sullivan. He imagined Bernie under the bed, clamping his hands over his mouth to keep from giggling. Posing for pictures with one of Alicia's friends to pretend he was a gay man. Installing a video camera in the apartment so they could sell the footage later on the Internet. If this had been one of Alicia's movies, then Sullivan would push her aside right now and lean under that bed to make the big reveal. Alicia would cry, but not really, just those awful gasps and hiccups, and then she and Bernie would reveal their whole plot. They'd confess to it all, the big sham, how all of Alicia's exotic costumes were part of it, too, a way to make it look like Sullivan was bringing different women to the apartment, like some kind of sleazy prostitute scam. They were framing him, for some reason Sullivan hadn't even known about. An inheritance, maybe.

If this was one of Alicia's movies, Sullivan would slap her across the face. Not enough to really hurt, just to sting, just to get some of his dignity back. And then he'd steal something valuable from both of them and use it to start a new life, a new identity somewhere else.

Instead, he was just a guy being broken up with by a girl who was all wrong for him anyway. Instead, he was just a guy wearing someone else's suit. Not really there. Somewhere else.

Half the Distance
to the Goal Line

There was a time when all of us wanted to be like Jack and Diane. It didn't matter that we didn't really like them. It didn't even matter that we sometimes made fun of their names, same as the Top 40 song that was popular for all those years. They were clichés just like that song—popular, good-looking, initials in a heart carved on the side of a tree. And we worshipped them.

Jack (his full name was Jackson, but really no one ever called him that except maybe his dad when he was pissed at him) was a varsity football player, and though Diane was no cheerleader, she did have a lot of leads in the high school chorus. The freshman and sophomore girls aimed for perfect imitation—how to get our hair to stay in such luscious curls all day long, cuff our pants at just the right length, choose just enough jewelry to stand out but not look like we were trying too hard. And the guys—well, we just stepped back against our lockers, watching Jack walk down the halls, football in hand. Jack and Diane were the standards to live up to, the topic of conversation worth having.

And then in later years, of course, there were the fights. Big, spectacular cinematic displays that got retold in a kind of Telephone Game, over and over again in the halls. Diane spilling beer on Jack's head at a house party. Jack speeding off, tires squealing, from Diane's house, rolling over the curb in his hurry to get away from her. Slammed phones, love notes shoved in lockers, rumors of a pregnancy, and then always, when the smoke cleared, the picturesque image of the two of them walking side by side through the lunch room, their hands in the back pockets of each other's Levis Five-Oh-Ones.

Everyone in school knew it was clichéd. We all should've known, anyway. But there was something about Jack and Diane that made you believe. Even when they won Homecoming King and Queen—because, yes, that too happened—and someone switched their first dance song from "Open Arms" to "Jack and Diane" as a joke, even then it all seemed somehow fitting. And they took it in stride, awkwardly twirling to the fast beat, the hand claps, while John Cougar told them it wasn't going to be like this forever, that they needed to make it all last as long as they could.

So they did. Long after we graduated, tossed caps in the air and opened 40s in our parents' basements, long after we got jobs, got married, started paying for flood insurance and forgot all about Jack and Diane, those two were still swaying back and forth in that gym. They played that song until the record broke, 'til the tape ran out, and later they bought the CD as an upgrade. They played it until it wasn't very fun anymore. And even after that.

***

Let's catch up with them now, heading down Central Street. It's late-summer, 2007. Next year will be our tenth high school reunion, and everyone will be talking about how there's still no ring on Diane's finger. Jack is fiddling with the radio buttons, trying to find an AM station that actually carries the Penn State football game. He doesn't want to miss any of it in the ten minutes it takes to drive to the house of his cousin Jen and her husband Bobby, where they will have dinner. Diane has even made a cake for the occasion.

Diane is fiddling with her dress, absentmindedly rubbing the soft silk of the skirt between her fingers. She's not happy with her outfit— she was trying something different, something softer than she normally goes for and now she feels a little ridiculous, a little too old for the bright yellow flower print. She had even tossed a light, white scarf around her neck that Jen had given her as a birthday present several years ago. Diane never wears scarves. She doesn't like the way they make her neck feel, and now, as we watch, she pulls it off and shoves it into her tiny purse where later it will mask the sound of her phone ringing.

"We're going to be late again, and I just know that Jen's going to say something about it," Diane says, mostly to herself.

"Shh, shh, they're going to pass it here." This is Jack, of course, and if his voice seems deeper, gruffer, than you remember it, it's probably from the years of working at Jiffy Lube and breathing in all that gasoline and oil.

Penn State is losing by three to Michigan in the fourth quarter with five minutes left in the game. Over the radio, a monotone voice crackles through the static. "Jensen's on the fly, he's back, he's got an opening on the left and it's a wide one out to Patson, complete pass, down to the five-yard line."

"Yes!" Jack claps his hands together once, pumps a fist in the air. He is thinking of that feeling, his team in the red zone. He's thinking about lining up, slamming hard into whatever body happened to be in front of him, protecting his quarterback, hearing the thunder in his ears. Truly, predictably, nothing like it, folks.

Jack pulls up to Jen and Bobby's house and cuts the engine. He is waiting, leaning forward, staring at the radio. Diane looks up at the house, a pretty two-story on the corner, and wonders if they have a buyer yet.

Jack reaches over and fluffs Diane's hair until she squeals and pulls away. He laughs. "Come on, babe, chill out. We're going to dinner, not to the firing squad."

"I know, I know. It's just…" she stops, trying to decide what to say. "Well, you know."

He does. That's the beauty of being together for so long. You can read each other's minds, finish each other's sentences.

"They've got it in the bag now," Jack says, which makes Diane roll her eyes and start chewing her fingernails out of nervousness. He might've been the football player in high school, might've started the entire four years and might've been one of the guys responsible for the team's run to States his junior year, but she knows a lot about football. Enough to know that if Penn State scores now, with three minutes left, there is still a whole lot of stuff that could happen.

"Quarterback sneak," Jack mumbles. He presses his fingers together as if in prayer. The announcer calls the play—a swift pass down the middle of the field. Just as the receiver catches it, and the announcer and Jack in unison scream, "Touchdown!," Jen opens the front door of the house, pot holder in her right hand, and begins beckoning to them.

**

The deal is, Diane doesn't really like Jen. And Jack doesn't really like Jen's husband Bobby. But Jen and Jack are family. And Jen just happened to mess around with, and then marry, one of the only guys on their high school football team that Jack hates.

And yet, pretenses are pretenses, and so when Jen greets Diane with a big hug and genuine seeming "hello," Diane smiles warmly and clasps Jen's hands. Bobby gives Jack a hearty slap-five handshake and asks him what beer will wet his whistle.

"Boss," Bobby calls Jack by his nickname still, "glad you could make it. Wish we'd done this more often." The 100 percent cashmere Ralph Lauren sweater vest that Bobby has deliberately worn for this evening is completely lost on Jack, who thinks a designer shirt is one that doesn't have a beer logo on the front.

"Is it me or is it already starting to get darker earlier?" Jen asks Diane, navigating her to the kitchen, and Diane cannot help but wonder if this is some kind of dig on them being late. But before she can answer, Jen has moved on to another topic. "So, we were going to grill out," Jen continues, her eyes batting up and down, thick mascara clumping at the ends of her lashes. "But the grill died on Bobby yesterday, just up and kicked it. Which we thought, whatever, it's less we have to move now, right?"

"Congratulations," Diane says. "I'm so happy for you guys."

"Thanks, love," Jen says. She's eternally been the girl who wants to lose 10 pounds. Even in high school, Jen never lost that baby fat, as the years passed that ten has stretched to twenty, thirty pounds. Jen has a pretty face, spends tons of money on highlights and layers, and in the summer she can get away with spaghetti strap tank tops because her shoulders are thin and tan. And yet her body follows nearly perfectly the curves of the Bartlett pear sitting in the fruit bowl in the counter. When she bends down to retrieve two bottles of Miller Lite from the bottom shelf of the refrigerator, it makes Diane a little sick.

"I brought a cake," Diane says, setting the box on the counter.

"Oh, you made it?" Jen says distractedly. "Mom's always saying how good your cakes are."

"Aunt Rita says you like chocolate raspberry," Diane says, waiting, but Jen doesn't even bother to glance over at the cake. It took Diane the entire afternoon to make that cake, so we know she's a little pissed about this, same way she used to get pissed at the drama girls who never said thank you when Diane drove them home after practice.

Jen passes the beers to Diane. "Would you mind?"

Diane sets her purse down on the kitchen chair and takes the beers into the living room for the boys. She makes a mental note to remember to check her phone. Her friend Jill's idea, this phone "interview" with Mr. Todd Lucas, owner of some fancy bakery in New York City that Jill's firm insures. He is heading to France for two weeks, but supposedly has agreed to call Diane from the airport before his flight to chat about the opening he has. Diane has her doubts.

The guys immediately open the bottles and stand in front of the TV to watch the end of the game. "I've got that Sunday ticket deal for the NFL," Bobby tells Jack, spouting off all the perks and, of course, the price. Jack just nods, concentrating on the TV where Michigan, Diane sees with a cringe, has run the ball back up the field and is threatening to score once again. Penn State was penalized for holding, which advanced Michigan half the distance to the goal line with a first down. Four opportunities to score.

***

"So the douchebag that wanted my job is giving me shit now," Bobby is telling Jack. "He's filing a complaint with Human Resources that they didn't consider Affirmative Action during the interview process."

"Is he black?"

"Nah, Hispanic," Bobby says, moving his fingers in air quotes.

"That covers them?"

Bobby shrugs. "I guess so. Any kind of minority."

"The rate stuff's going, we'll soon be the minority."

"Hills to bills, I've had three more years' experience and just closed out a 1.5 million deal. And he's telling me he's more qualified because of his taco-making skills? Pfft."

This is it, Jack sees. The fuckers have run down the clock enough to win now. A slew of Penn State fans are filing out of the stands, heads down. Time clock management. It gets them every time. You think they'd learn.

Bobby is still on his long story about the job, and Jack interrupts. "So what's your new title again?"

"Regional account manager," Bobby says proudly, setting it off with a burp. Jack has no idea what that means or what Bobby does at the bank, and he doesn't much care. He just knows this new promotion is taking Bobby and Jen to Philadelphia for a big-shot chance that no one will shut up about. Bobby always does it better than anyone else.

"Ah fuck," Bobby says. "They're going to lose."

"Yeah, I know," Jack says. "It's still early in the season, though."

"Stupid assholes can't play defense worth a damn."

"It was the offense. They scored too soon."

"Well, scoring ain't a bad thing, Boss." Bobby laughs. "But if your defense can't hold 'em back, well, that's where the problem lies, eh?"

Jack smiles, itching to punch him. It's always been like this. Mr. Wide Receiver back in high school. He remembers Bobby getting in his face. "I won this game for you assholes and you pay me back by leaving a wide fucking hole down the middle?" And then later, once Bobby had gone on to college, even when he'd sat on the bench for Penn State an entire year, never once getting field time, he managed to blame it on someone else. The coach, the schedule. And then when he did play, and a cornerback slammed into his legs, busting out his knee, it ruined his career in about five seconds.

"Whatever you say, dude," Jack says, and holds up his bottle. "Can I have another?"

***

As they sit down to dinner, outside on the patio where they use generic bug spray to try to keep the mosquitoes away, swear to God, out of Jen's tiny iPod speakers Diane can hear that John Cougar song on low. "Life goes on, long after the thrill of living is gone." It almost has to be a joke set up by Jen on purpose, but when Diane studies her, she can't find any trace of smugness. Jen is dishing out heaps of potato salad on everyone's plate and chattering about health insurance. They're all a little drunk, and Diane realizes she's the only one paying attention to the music. She hates that stupid song.

Jen's using the defunct grill as a wobbly side table to put the beans and napkins on. They are sitting on tiny lawn chairs, fine enough size for the women, but Jack's knees come up to his chest and he keeps having to adjust so he doesn't topple the whole table over.

"So the house we got in Philly is in a really good school district," Jen is telling Diane. "It's ranked like fifth in the state or something."

Diane nods, and takes a large swig of her beer. "That's probably good for the property values then." She's once again studying Jen's face for any signs of spite, but Jen seems truly in her own world. Lucky, lucky her.

Jen shrugs, glances shyly at Bobby, who's in the middle of a story, and then she leans in towards Diane. "We'll probably start trying this fall."

Diane feels a little sick to her stomach. She wants to change the subject but she is at a loss as to how. There's only one thing that makes her feel better here and that is imagining all the weight this woman will gain when she's pregnant, ingesting everything within arm's reach. Don't judge Diane, she feels guilty enough.

"Eff that game," Jack says loudly, and Diane turns with relief to him.

"They're gonna be shitty this year," Bobby is saying. "Sometimes it happens. You can't always have a winning year."

"So Michigan scored on the penalty?" Diane asks, though she already knows.

"Who cares," Jen mutters.

"What do you think?" Jack says.

Diane shrugs. "Sorry." She pauses, then says, "You know, I really hate that rule."

"Which?" Bobby asks, since Jack is preoccupied with trying to fit his entire chicken leg into his mouth.

"Half the distance to the goal line. It's weird. You could keep going and going and going and yet you'll never reach it."

Bobby whistles, grinning. "Whoa, that's deep Diane." He leans over and knocks his knuckles lightly against her head. "Watch out or your ears will start smoking there."

He's always tried to flirt with Diane, ever since high school, and he's always failed pretty miserably at it. Still, there was a time, a brief time before Bobby started dating Jen, where Bobby and Diane were really close friends, and it is that time that allows Diane to forgive him for his obnoxiousness. Bobby laughs loudly, too loudly, and then when he finally contains himself he grabs his beer and holds it up.

"Time for a toast! To Philly," Bobby toasts himself, and they all chime in, clinking bottles together like one big happy family. The wind starts to gust up and Diane is thinking of possibilities. She has her purse with her, draped against the back of her chair, and she checks her watch again.

"To the future," Jen adds, winking at Diane. "You never know what it might hold."

Diane feels her chest getting hot, wondering how Jen knows about the phone interview, but then she realizes Jen is just on her old crusade. Jack knows it too, and it irritates him. His cousin is much too nosy for her own good, and part of him hopes they're miserable in their new place. But just a tiny part of him, really. He's always been a pretty generous person underneath all the guy-ness, which is why we think Diane has tolerated him for so long.

"Cuz, you should really worry about your own situation," he says.

"What do you mean?" Jen asks, picking a gnat out of her untouched water glass and flicking it on the deck.

He shakes his head in a way that he imagines to be more scornful than it actually is. "Your hints. About everything."

"Well, sometimes you need a push, that's all."

"Well, sometimes not everyone is in the same situation you are." And they shouldn't be, Jack is thinking. In this town, people don't leave. We stay, vote for the wrong people, bitch about the potholes, get married, drink pink champagne, and worry about the future. Then we have babies that grow up and get married and stay here and bitch. Circle of Central PA Life, my friends, and it really gets under Jack's collar that Bobby and Jen are breaking the rules.

"Oh God, Jack, honestly. How many years has it been?" Jen asks, trying to be casual, but her shaking hands are giving her away. Diane remembers a moment at Jen and Bobby's wedding several years ago when, passing her in the hallway, Jen had stopped Diane, clutched her cheek in her hand and spoke softly, "Oh, honey, don't worry that you didn't catch my flowers. I'm sure you'll be next."

***

"Yeah, buddy, you ever think about going back to school?" Bobby's saying now to Jack, dishing out the advice like Jen serves her cheeseburger casserole, piling heaps and heaps of gooey smugness. He tips his beer their way and winks. Yep, he winks. "There are all kinds of new programs now, night classes and shit. You could get a degree in a year or two."

Diane rolls her eyes. "I think Jack's doing fine, Bobby."

Bobby shrugs. "Hey baby, I'm not trying to get up in your boy's grid. I'm just sayin'."

Diane feels her face get hot. "Saying what? Do you know that Jack got promoted recently, too?"

"Diane—" Jack starts to say, but Diane just gets louder.

"No, he didn't tell you because he doesn't like to brag, doesn't like to go off about all his accomplishments, but he's the manager there now." She smiles at Jack, but he looks past her, his face pinched.

"Jesus, Jack, that's great," Jen says. "But that wasn't even what I was talking about. I meant you two. Ever thought about settling down, you know, for real?"

"Oh for fuck's sake, Jen," Jack erupts.

Diane stands suddenly. "Excuse me, I need to use the bathroom."

"Oh Diane, don't run. God." Jen looks up at her. "Don't you ever want a ring on your finger?"

Jack snorts. "A ring? Please." He nods at Bobby. "I see what happened to him when he married you. We aren't going that road."

Jen sits up straighter, her eyebrows pinched, and Diane thinks, *serves you right*. She gets up from the table and takes one long look at the beans on her way inside. She has the urge to smear them all over Jen's tiny perky face.

"Oh come on," Bobby is saying. "It's not that bad."

"Oh, thank you very much," Jen says, her voice leaking into the hallway as Diane opens the bathroom door, presses her head against the cool bathroom mirror, and breathes. She can't hear them any-more.

Shit. She forgot her purse, her phone. Mr. Lucas is probably calling her now, or will be soon. Mr. Lucas. What kind of name is that, anyway? It sounds stupid to her, sounds like some guy in a stupid movie set in a stupid place far away. She thinks it's so ridiculous she laughs out loud at herself. "Yeah, right, Diane Lynn Shushinski. Just who the hell do you think you are?"

Diane collects herself, splashes some water on her face. When she comes out, Bobby is in the hall, leaning against the wall waiting for her. "They're still bickering out there, like little hens," he says, and his voice is slightly slurred. Everything seems slow motion.

"God, I wish they would just drop it," Diane says, fluffing her hair nervously.

Bobby smiles, pushes himself off the wall toward her. "Diane, you've still got the most beautiful set of eyes I've ever seen on any woman."

She flushes, presses her thumbs together. "Thanks, Bobby," she barely says, and pushes by him, up the stairs and into the kitchen, where she can hear Jen's high-pitched voice rushing hurriedly in her own defense.

***

Jack has always liked the song "I Am a Rock." He thinks of the words now as he settles into his too-small chair, tipping back his sixth bottle of beer. It's just barely September, and we all know what he's feeling: honestly, what can be better than this, sitting outside with a nice buzz and the night breeze around you, confident in your own view of the world, a rock, an island. He looks at Jen and Bobby and he pities them and their little views of the way things should be. He always has. He remembers going over to his aunt and uncle's house when he was a kid, and how Jen always wanted to play house. She cooked dinner and he pretended to come home from work. She really enjoyed setting the table and asking him how his day was.

As if she's messing with him, Jen claps her hands. "We've got dessert!" she says. "Diane's cake! Who wants some?"

"I think I want to play some football," Jack says suddenly, feeling it wash over him in cold certainty.

Bobby laughs. "You're nuts."

"No, come on," Jack says again, his eyes darkening. "Just one pass. For old times sake."

Jen laughs nervously, her eyes focused on Bobby in a way that Diane can't read. "You boys and your games," she says, trailing off at the end. Diane refuses to look at her. She wants her to hang dry on this one. And Diane knows, with a vicious smug satisfaction, that Jack will prevail. We all know it, too, though we can't help feeling a little sorry for Bobby, who's surely regretting the sweater vest right about now.

"All right, just one," Bobby says, setting down his bottle next to the grill. He walks inside, comes back a few minutes later with a football. Jack grins. He knows Bobby can't bear to look like a pussy in front of him. All those times at practice, in the locker room, the challenges Bobby never backed down from, the fights he went for even when he knew he'd lose. Bobby tosses Jack the football.

"Go out," Jack says, and Bobby starts running. He looks funny to Diane, a banker running in his pressed khakis. She has a bad feeling, the way we used to all feel hauling six-packs up to the old coal mine, but she thinks if she doesn't pay much attention, if she just goes along with it, everything will be all right.

"He's such an asshole," Jen mutters. Diane doesn't know who she's referring to.

"Farther, farther," Jack shouts, until Bobby gets almost to the back fence. "Now!" he says and throws a perfect spiral right into Bobby's open arms. And his daddy always said he should've been a quarterback.

Bobby catches it and starts running back. If his knee is bothering him, he doesn't show it. He has his hands up in the air, holding the football like he is about to spike it, like the world is about to leap to their feet in wonder, when Jack lunges at him.

***

Let's freeze this for a moment, the two guys in motion, about to collide. There is something about this moment that seems inevitable, sure, we felt that from the moment Jack and Diane stepped into the house. Too much history there. We know some of it. We know enough to know that even though this is happening, it's not really going to change much. You can't change all those years, all the little hurts, the vicious rumors, the day-to-day decisions that people make that pile up, one on top of the other like a very elaborate, sickeningly sweet cake. You just have to take a small slice and eat it.

Here's what we know: that Jack, at this moment, has had three-too-many beers. And he's dying to wipe that smug smile off Bobby's face. He wants to knock him down, show him they aren't on the same team any-more. That they were never on the same team. He's thinking about high school—we all do when we get together in groups—and he's thinking about Diane.

We don't really know the whole story. There were lots of rumors, and after awhile around here rumors become fact. We know that some of Diane's friends said she was in trouble, of the nine-month variety. We know she and Jack broke up for awhile around that time, for longer than their other break-ups, for long enough that we worried that might really be it. We know she and Bobby were good friends then, that she would trust him to help her. But we can only imagine, along with Jack, what really happened the day she might've gone to do it. Bobby's hand on Diane's back, comforting her as they walk to the clinic. Diane signing papers, meeting the doctor, hands sweating, thin hospital gown fraying at the edges and curling up around her calves—we imagine it as surreal, we imagine she may have pulled away as though she was watching a movie, watching all this happening to someone else.

Then Bobby pacing the waiting room, collecting her when it's over, driving her home, maybe even kissing her cheek, wishing somehow it was different. Wishing maybe he was the one. We don't know what happened when Diane finally found herself alone, curled up on the bed with her giant stuffed panda, staring at the walls covered in Bryan Adams and Christian Slater posters that only a few of us privileged folks had ever seen. We're not sure who she told, or even who we ever heard it from in the first place. We don't know how she feels now.

That's the stuff we don't talk about when we all get together. That's the stuff we only speculate at home, in bed in the dark with our wives, kids sleeping in the next room, water leaking in the bathtub. That's when we say it aloud, justifying our own decisions maybe—the real reason we think Jack won't marry Diane.

We do know, however, that when Jack throws himself into Bobby's middle out there in the backyard, he wants to hurt him. He wants to break bone.

***

The two of them crash loudly into the grill and fall to the ground. Jack feels the crush of a beer bottle pressing into his skin and it feels good.

Jen screams. It takes Diane longer to react and by the time she stands, the guys have rolled away from each other. Jack is groaning, and Diane can see blood on the back of his shirt. Bobby is holding his knee with one hand and with the other he's still clutching the stupid football.

"What the fuck?" Jen shouts, her face so red it is almost purple. "What is wrong with you guys? What is wrong?"

"I'm fine," Bobby says, but he isn't and they can all see it.

"Jesus Christ, you guys will never grow the fuck up," Jen screams now, and in her pinched face Diane can see her clearly, her bumpy cheeks and thin lips, that small chin that makes her look defensive all the time, all that makeup she uses and always has used, even in high school, how jealous she (and all of us) always were of Diane's perfect skin. The way she always mocked her with, *maybe she's born with it, maybe it's Maybeline* as though by making fun of Diane it would put them on an even plane, make Bobby stop looking at her like that when he thought Jen wasn't watching.

Diane pulls the broken bits of glass from Jack's back. He groans, burps. He feels heavy, large, a massive sack of a burden. Her burden. If he was really hurt, she wonders how the heck she would ever lift him into the car to drive him to the hospital. It overwhelms her in a way she hasn't felt in a very long time—the idea of being responsible for someone else—and Diane feels like leaping off the side of the deck and running until her legs fall off.

Jen is still yelling, now through blubbery tears. She has a cordless phone in her hand and waves it around talking about calling an ambulance.

"Will you just shut up?" Diane says, even though we know what she really wants to say is: *Do you realize how much better you have it, you dumb bitch?*

"No one ever gets by me," Jack says. He sits up, smacks his thigh. Somewhere in the distance, they all hear a loud rumble from some young punk gunning his motorcycle's engine. "No one. You might think you have, but I know it."

Diane sits back on her heels. Somewhere, underneath all the shouting and confusion, she thinks she might hear the chipper beeping of her phone, the electronic tinny version of a rock song popular many years ago, but she's not really sure, and anyway, it's too far away.

The Oregon Trail

The Opposition

We left at the beginning of summer, figuring at least three months of good weather. We packed up what we could in the CRV. We had our baby, our camera, and our AAA membership. I quit my job at the dealership outright. Craig wasn't teaching until the fall, so we had a safety net in case we needed to come back.

We left because our apartment, and the world, felt small. The only new friends we had were parents who talked endlessly about the safety regulations of car seats and the color of their baby's poop. We left because the president wasn't going to get re-elected. We left because someone set fire to the playground near our house. We left because we started fighting clichés—chores, snoring, the cost of cable.

We left the cats with trusted friends, the bonsai tree with my dad.

We left because that's what people do when they are afraid.

***

It was Craig's idea to follow the Oregon Trail, albeit backwards. It was something, anyway. And we used to play that game, which I hated because my family always got sick and died, while Craig's family forged through the fucking country and founded a city. He planned and plotted and they thrived.

So the Oregon Trail it was. I wanted to see cattle, snorting, grazing free-range cattle just doing their thing out on open fields. I wanted to be somewhere where you could see for ten miles without a building getting in the way. I wanted to stand in the wind and let the dust settle in my hair. It sounded romantic. It sounded like just what we needed.

***

We drove for long periods of time, singing along to the radio until that got annoying. The day was hot, the windows down. Around mid-day we stopped at a Farmer's Market alongside the road. I had to wake Dru. We wandered. At one stand, a farmer was selling blueberries. I bought a pint and shared it with Dru. He loved blueberries. "Boo ber, boo ber," he'd say, holding out his fat fingers for more.

***

I started to feel sick around late afternoon and finally asked Craig to stop. The sun was hot on my head. It felt like it could burn right through me. I vomited hard on the side of the road. The blueberries. The desert looked unforgiving out there and I imagined suddenly those early pio-neers, out here in wagons and petticoats, paving the way in the desert with its rocks and dangerous plants and animals.

Dru cried inconsolably, like the way he had when he'd been colicky. We kept driving because we weren't sure what else to do. He shit out the blueberries, diaper after diaper, until we had to stop at an all-night CVS to buy more.

I sat in the back and sang "The Rainbow Connection," though I only knew the first verse. Craig wanted me to google the rest. "Some things we just don't always have to know," I snapped at him.

***

Saving dollars meant crappy motels that we called "vintage" to make ourselves feel better. We were never good at road trips. I'd forgotten the travel crib sheets and Craig kept second-guessing the route. One week, then two, then three. We began to get on each other's nerves. The air dried out my contacts, sandpaper in the eyes. The car seat made Dru's thighs sweat. He giggled like a leprechaun whenever I reached back and yanked on his big toe. "More play." We listened to books on tape. Craig started eating Pop Tarts right out of the silvery package. I kept thinking of the crumbs everywhere at our feet.

***

The car overheated somewhere just past the Red Desert in Wyoming. We sat in the pitch dark and waited for the tow truck from AAA to find us.

The lights of the pick-up truck that came up behind us felt like flood-lights. The kids stopped beside us, blocking the road, two teenagers with bandannas covering their hair, blasting country music. I recognized the song—something about jumping into the fire to really experience life.

The kid in the passenger seat looked over. His smile was like peeling back a can of Friskies—cold, sharp, metallic, with a whiff of something foul underneath.

***

When I told my mother I was marrying Craig, she frowned in that disapproving-but-I'm-not-going-to-say-it-out-loud way. "Are you sure that's what you want?"

"Ma? Of course. What kind of reaction is that?"

She shrugged. "It's just that…well," she trailed off.

My father finished it for her. "The man knows too much about flowers," he said. "No man should know that much about flowers."

***

"You havin' some kind a problem here?" one of the boys yelled over. He had a can of Yoo-Hoo in his hand.

"No, everything's fine," Craig said in a higher tone than normal. "Thanks."

"Doesn't look fine," the boy said. His friend, the driver, snickered. He turned down the music, and his friend leaned out of the window to look in our car. Eyes flickered on Dru. Go ahead, look at him again, I thought. I will go for your eyes first. Thrust my thumbs as hard as I can through that pulp and wash out the bits later in a 7-Eleven sink.

"Tow truck's on its way," Craig said. "Should be here any minute."

"Right, right," Yoo-Hoo said. The driver revved the engine. It echoed out into the desert.

***

Craig grew up in Brooklyn with Jewish parents who ate pork. I grew up in Seattle, where we lived, where it always rained and smelled like fish. Craig and I bonded in college over Westerns. Our first date was to see *The Good, the Bad, and the Ugly* at the Gateway Theater for Classics Wednesday. Craig brought an airplane bottle of vodka and spiked our soda. He was working on his thesis at the time and pointed out the names of all the desert plants to me. I didn't mind.

Later it evolved into a drinking game. We'd watch any kind of cowboy movie—the only rule was you had to do a shot for a shot. We liked the guns, the horses, the morals.

All we ever wanted was simplicity, green grass, straight whiskey.

Instead we got a two-bedroom, fifteenth floor apartment in the heart of Seattle, where you could see the Needle in the smallest bedroom window if you pressed your face hard to the glass and looked left. We got jobs in the city and a newspaper subscription. We got pregnant.

***

"Got a joke for ya," Yoo-Hoo said.

"Pardon me?" Craig said. He never talked like that, pardon me. It made him sound like an old man, white and weak.

"What do you call a monkey with a bomb?"

"What?"

"Did you not hear me?"

"I don't know," Craig said. I could tell he wanted to roll his window back up. I imagined him doing it and the guys shooting a bullet right through it. Bam.

No one really wants a cowboy, I used to tell my friend Mindy, who always seemed to fall for anyone with a drawl and a drinking problem. Those kind of guys leave you for bigger, noble purposes. They work too hard, or they die too young, or they have wandering eyes and smell like cow shit.

"You gotta guess, man. That's the whole point." Yoo-Hoo was getting fidgety, twisting around in his seat, cracking his can between his fist.

I kept looking back at the baby. He was sleeping still, somehow, through all this racket. When we first brought him home, we used to tiptoe around the house during his naps, careful not to clang a pot or close a door too fast. Then one day the neighbors above us had their flooring replaced and Dru was so still through it all I went in his room and rested my hand on his back until it rose with his breath.

"Just guess," I said, words spitting out of me like shrapnel. "Just fucking guess."

Craig looked at me, his eyes blinking crazily. He was flushed. I could tell that in the dark of the desert. Like he'd just run ten miles.

"Ape shit," Craig said. The guy closest to us leaned out, and Craig said it louder. "Ape shit."

"Ape shit," he said to the driver. They repeated it again, laughing. The driver hit his palm against the steering wheel. "Ape shit." They nodded. "That's pretty good, man."

Craig laughed, too, a little too hard. Yoo Hoo crushed the can with his fist and tossed it into the road. He tipped his head once, twice at us. The driver revved the engine again, tore off, rubber screaming on the hot pavement. He held his horn down for what seemed like miles. If I concentrate hard enough, I can still hear it echoing over the mountain, a wailing, dying sound.

***

We found some small motel with a sombrero sign and a built-in pool. The water was inky and streaked with the reds and blues of the neon hat sign.

We put Dru in the travel crib between our beds and went outside to stick our feet in the water, the baby monitor between us. It was quiet except for the hum of a generator.

"This is the life," Craig said.

"If only we had some Boone's wine or what was that stuff—Zima?"

"Classy."

Neither of us would admit what we were thinking: that gentle way our couch back home gave way to your body weight after a long hard day. The homeless guy with the missing finger who sat in the alley across the street. Sesame bread from scratch. The fact that those boys could've slit all our throats and left us bleeding it out in the dirt and Craig could do fuck-all to stop it.

"I googled it, by the way," I said.

Craig looked over at me, skimmed his fingers along the water's surface. "What?"

"It's a baboom. A monkey with a bomb. A baboom."

The motel manager opened the office door, dragging a garbage bin behind her. She had one of those old lady housecoats on with pastel floral print. She coughed, not bothering to cover her mouth, and looked over at us.

"Watch yer bums," she called. "The scorpions come out at night."

✷ ✷ ✷

You don't arrive at the Great Plains. They come to you. Suddenly you realize you're in the middle of those patches of squares you usually only see from airplanes. Suddenly you realize how inconsequential you and your vintage washed jeans are to the earth. It's been there. It couldn't care less what you want, what you desire, where you came from, and where you're going.

It was windy and hot. I made Craig pull over on the side of the road so we could get out. Dru felt like a space heater in my arms. He kept squinting his eyes to block out the sun, kicking his bare feet into my belly. "Down, down," he wanted, and I imagined just watching him run for miles and still being able to see his little toddler trot.

And that was it—that's what was bothering me. The openness. Back in Seattle, where the buildings sprouted up all around you, a long flat landscape of nothing seemed exciting. But here now, it was all laid out in front of you. Predictable, like your life as a novel that you already peeked at and read the ending.

Miles away—maybe twenty, thirty we could see some clouds gathering. The rainstorm approached rapidly, like a massive swarm of bees, darkening the fields beneath it, heading our way.

I thought about those cowboys. Those pioneer fools so many years ago, rocking across this place in their rickety wagons with their dysentery and their snake bites. What they would've thought of us here, me with my cup of coffee and Ray Ban sunglasses and Craig with his sleeping pills and digital recorder. I imagined us all those years ago, hunched over Craig's desktop computer playing that game. Naming the kids in our family that died of snakebites, fell off cliffs, drowned in the rivers. Craig trying to tell me what move to make and me spitefully doing the opposite.

The storm was getting closer. We could smell it now, the wet dirt smell where heat and cold mixed. We'd have to wait it out in the car, the only shelter in sight. There was nowhere else to go.

"So is it all you thought?" Craig asked. His hair was tossing about and he looked thin, like the storm might just scoop him right up. It occurred to me that sometimes being a true pioneer meant protecting the ones with whom you were taking the journey.

"Oh yeah," I lied. "It's exactly what I imagined."

Other People's Houses

Their real estate agent is so pleasant. She has boys of her own. Three boys! Imagine that. "Ha ha ha. You'll never sleep again. Just get ready to have your world turn upside down," she says. In a good way, of course. She hands Derek and Hannah each a shiny business card with edges sharp enough to draw blood. Mathilda Bee is her name, and her slogan on the business card reads: *I'll take the sting out of buying!* She squeezes Hannah's upper arm and sighs, then presses her thumbs to her temple. "My word, the beauty of a life I'm imagining for you two—you three. The beauty!" She calms down, leans forward again. "So are we thinking three or four bedrooms?"

***

Derek knows nothing substantial about the guy Hannah fucked. He knows his name and his age and how she met him—the douche was renovating their apartment complex's gym. He could do more research but his therapist frowns on this. On the way out of the real estate agent's office he thinks, though, that perhaps once he and Hannah find a place he may make a bitter crack about how they can call Paul in to remodel the place and make it more "homey." He thinks about saying this and it feels to him like unleashing a wild pack of lions on her bones. But he just keeps quiet. He's supposed to be working on the anger.

"Should we have waited for her?" Hannah asks him after the second house is not only difficult to find but also a bust—a two-story little dump that looks like it would topple over if the Big Bad Wolf blew on it too hard. Mathilda Bee had offered to take them out next week, show them some places, but Derek had not wanted to waste any time and just asked for a list.

"What? And spoil this good time?" he says, laying on his horn as a car cuts in front of him. He knows he's being a jerk. It's like he can't help himself.

It's the Christmas carols that have been bothering him the most, bringing it all up again. Have you ever noticed how many Christmas songs are about being alone? He punches off the songs—"Last Christmas," "Blue Christmas," "Please Come Home for Christmas," even though he knows Hannah eats all that stuff up—the cookies and the music and the trees and all of it.

Most of all he hates the holiday traffic. They have already traveled the boulevard four times today for these stupid houses out in the West Bridge neighborhood and are now heading back toward Salmonville. You can't drive anywhere without going on the boulevard, which the city tries every year to spruce up by adding garlands and white lights in the bare trees. And of course the Santa—whose arm was broken off last year and who just hangs outside the hotel sort of lopsided—is supposed to add something nostalgic to the whole depressing picture.

"They really ought to replace him, don't you think?" Hannah says as if reading his mind.

He doesn't answer. He's thinking about how it wasn't always like this. When he was a kid, like every other kid, he loved the holidays, but now they were just there to torment him, to make him remember that you couldn't trust anyone, that you never really knew anyone. Now they are here to remind him that his marriage was as big of a sham as Santa himself—just an imagined magic he was fooled into believing in for a few years. But now he knows.

"How does a Santa lose an arm anyway?" Hannah says again, chewing on the skin around her index finger.

Out of nowhere, it starts to snow, flecks of lace that melt immediately upon hitting the windshield. "We'll call her when we get home," he says. "She can take us next weekend. Show us her secrets."

***

Hannah takes to calling the real estate agent Honey Bee to Derek, which is sometimes shortened to Ms. Bee or just Honey. Honey, in Hannah's mind, is the perfect family woman. She never makes mistakes, never strays. She is graying a little and gets her hair dyed professionally every six weeks, but her husband would adore her no matter how she looked. She is a little plump, but nothing to really gossip about, and she always wears clothes that look like blankets, big and sweeping in muted colors. Hannah thinks of her as one giant comfortable couch, and imagines that her boys slink up to her while watching TV and plant their heads between her breasts to fall asleep at night. She probably knows how to make jam.

Hannah would bet Honey also loves the downtown Christmas decorations. She and her three rambunctious boys and her little-too-large but loveable husband make a trek down there for an annual tradition of seeing the lights and getting hot chocolate at Clennson's. They wear matching sweaters, the boys, from the Gap or, if it is a tough year for real estate, Old Navy. She imagines the littlest of the boys, Ryan, likes his hot chocolate with extra marshmallows, and he asks the girl behind the counter for more more more, which is a little obnoxious but still cute if you like kids. They made a list for Santa. Most of them still believe in him, except the eldest is starting to have doubts. They have asked for boy technologies—Xboxes, iPhones, iPads, radio-controlled helicopters. They have not asked for guns or space aliens. They get Christmas pajamas to unwrap on Christmas Eve, and then Honey washes and dries them late that night so they can wear them on Christmas Day and not be itchy.

***

Today's first house sits in the middle of a cul de sac, and Hannah remembers an old co-worker of hers saying that living on a cul de sac is like being at the end of a fishing pole—shake shake shake all you want to, but you're always on display, always the worm dangling off the hook. The house seems dreary—Hannah doesn't even want to get out of the car. She wants to tell Honey Bee, who is already slamming the driver's side door, checking her folder of endless notes notes notes, to just forget about it, to drive on, but Hannah senses Derek thinks she is being picky, and so she resists.

There are not enough windows, which makes the house seem more like an old mom-and-pop store than a residence. Honey struggles with the lock box while Derek shakes the porch railings, testing for what? The front door squeaks and they enter, their eyes adjusting to the dimness, the smell of something old assaulting Hannah's nostrils.

She hates it more.

"So you have the living area off to the side here, opening into a hallway with the kitchen in the back," Honey Bee starts her trail of words, moving, pressing forward.

Death. Someone died here. Maybe right under Hannah's feet. She feels nauseated, the way she feels these days at the thought of eating or smelling refried beans. The furniture from the previous owners looks saggy, like beanbags that have lost half of their stuffing. A heavy, tan blackout curtain dwarfs the one small window in the living room. As if Honey knows, she walks quickly over and pushes it aside. "Let's get some light in here."

"Where are the light switches?" Derek asks quietly.

"New carpeting!" Honey points out.

Upstairs the smell gets worse but the features get better. Honey points out the marble bathroom countertops and claw-footed tub. "Newly remodeled," she says. Hannah wonders if Paul did the work, imagines him here on the floor, his jeans stained with dirt and sweat. Sometimes when they were lying in bed after sex she would find traces of dust in the sheets or under her nails. Even after a shower he kept shedding it.

Honey points out the walk-in closets and the built-in bookshelves. The rooms are small. On one wall is a painting of a duck in the middle of a pond. The trees surrounding the pond are bent inwards, threatening giant fingers trying to grasp something. The closet of the spare bedroom is filled with pastel suits, lace-collared button-down shirts, white nursing sneakers.

Hannah looks out the window. Imagines an older woman looking out on this spot—where is she now? Dead? On the street below, a white truck with a ladder drives by and Hannah thinks again of Paul. What if she never sees him again? She is okay with that, right? This is what she wants, this here with Derek, how it should be. Before she screwed up.

"You're not happy, right?" Honey Bee's voice, always so upbeat, startles Hannah.

"What?"

Honey, who apparently likes to touch Hannah, pats her shoulder, smiles. "Before you give up totally, you'll want to see the basement." She leads Hannah and Derek down a carpeted staircase where the stairs feel like they're slipping away, eroding on the edges from years of use. Honey flips on a light switch to flood the dark room with florescent light. "Look! A man cave," she says, smiling. "Imagine a pool table here. Or a bar. Or," she adds, glancing at Hannah's stomach, "a nice secluded play area for the little ones."

"I don't think this is quite what we're looking for." Hannah breathes, her hands resting on her stomach as if to protect the baby from the awful thought of having to live here.

"Yeah, it's a little…claustrophobic," Derek says, and Hannah is surprised at how good it feels for him to agree with her. On the way back up the stairs, she feels his hand on the small of her back.

***

The theater out in Franklin is the only one showing the new *Texas Chainsaw Massacre* remake. It isn't supposed to snow until the next morning, so Derek drives out there. The theater is nearly empty except for a few college-aged couples, thin, stupid girls thrusting their made-up faces into their boyfriend's North Face coats and pounding thick, fake-fur snowboots on the seat in front of them. It is, predictably, a terrible movie, though the one scene with the eyeballs is kind of cool.

Derek has been going to horror movies since the separation last year and now he can't stop. He goes mostly alone, though occasionally with a coworker Mindy. She is about eight years younger than him, and though nothing bad has happened, it feels kind of wrong and also deliciously dangerous. She calls him her "horror buddy," and even that seems stupid and yet kind of cool. Mindy wears mostly black and has a nose stud that sparkles in the dark theater and she laughs a little too hard if there is ever a scene involving or suggesting castration. He suspects she is a lesbian and this both disappoints and relieves him greatly.

He likes the classic B horror movies from the '80s, the slasher films that kill off hordes of teenagers. Mindy, back when he was still separated from Hannah, used to try to psychoanalyze him. "I get it, Derek. I totally get it. You like the morality, the code, of these movies. The ones that deserve it get killed. You're dumb, you get killed. You have sex when you aren't supposed to, you get hacked to pieces. The smart ones win. The moral ones win. They survive. They go home."

He lets her be right. He nods at the appropriate times. But it isn't true. It isn't why he likes those movies—it is much simpler than that. He likes them because he wants to watch stories about people whose lives are way more fucked up than his, whose luck is way worse. It makes him feel better to compare. It's why he watches the evening news, too, to count all the families, the victims, the downtrodden people for whom things really sucked pot. He is that selfish.

***

There is a senior center on the same block as Hannah's physical therapy practice, so on the way to work Hannah finds herself dodging around elderly people, her sturdy rubber boots squishing the slush on the sidewalks. She passes the bus stop each morning, and if the timing is right—and it usually is—she'll see the same people getting off the bus. The black lady with her small daughter, always holding hands, always in a hurry to school. The pear-shaped man with pink ear buds and a brown paper bag. The business suit. Occasionally she'll see a blind lady walking past, her thin white walking stick constantly swishing swishing back and forth. Hannah makes an arc around her, too, careful to avoid the stick.

The majority of the patients the practice serves are elderly. They also get construction workers with bad backs or knees and high school athletes who twisted something the wrong way.

It is just Hannah and Frances today, and their patient load is steady. Hannah treats Bernie, an older woman with bursitis in both knees. She is wearing a Christmas sweater with cats. If Hannah doesn't watch her constantly, the woman cheats, skipping leg lifts, and so Hannah stands with her, counting.

"You must be excited about the holidays," Hannah says to pass the time. "Are you traveling?"

"No," Bernie says. She has bad teeth and a hairstyle that makes her look ten years older than she really is. As she lays on her back on the table, the extra skin around her chin spreads out like putty. "It's just me and my daughter these days, so we don't really make a big deal out of it. You know how it is."

"That sounds nice," Hannah says. She is picturing this woman and her grown daughter sitting in a cold dining room, eating take-out. It makes her want to cry.

As if she knows, Frances catches Hannah's eye and smiles. She says to the woman, "Oh Bernie, you know you'll end up running all over town visiting all your friends, so don't give me that."

Bernie smiles, does a half-lift with her leg. "We'll see if they deserve my pumpkin roll this year."

When she gets a break, Hannah goes back to the kitchen and heats up a frozen pizza. Frances is already there, drinking a coke and flipping through a catalog.

Frances manages the practice and she's also Hannah's best friend even though sometimes Hannah dislikes her overbearing nature, her tendency to be too blunt. Still, she was the only person Hannah was able to talk to about the affair.

"You know Bernie is like the whore of her street."

"Frances!"

"It's true. I saw you getting all sad with her woe-is-me, but she's got a new boyfriend like every month. She had 'em lined up before her husband was even cold on the slab."

Frances never worries about saying shocking things. All the old men love her. She tells them lewd jokes, makes them laugh, gets them to do another round of weights before they even know enough to whine about it.

"How's the house hunting going?"

"Fine."

"What's wrong?"

"It's just so overwhelming. Looking at all these places. How do you know which one's the right one?"

"Is this really what you want?"

"What? A house? Of course. Why?"

Frances shrugs. "Just making sure. You know, with all that's happened."

"Frances, I'm having his child. He's my husband. Besides, you know all that other stuff is just, well, just stupid."

Hannah blames Frances for starting the whole thing, though she would never tell her that. But last fall, over a year ago, when Hannah told her that she thought the contractor in their apartment building was flirting with her, Frances had immediately gotten interested. Which had led to a discussion about just how many men Hannah had slept with (a low number, less than five if you really need to know), and Frances had laughed—Hannah can still remember that laugh, like a cracked whip between them—and said, "My word, you're like a prude! No wonder you can't tell when a man is flirting with you!"

***

Hannah has taken up crocheting. She enjoys holding the needle, wrapping and twisting and stabbing the yarn. She's trying to make baby booties that look like whales, but following the pattern while Derek's watching his cold case TV shows makes her lose track, mess up her counting.

She's sure Honey Bee knows how to crochet and knit. She probably holds her own yarn classes, for free, in her rec room in the finished basement. She teaches the neighbors popcorn stitches and knitting in the round, and they all ooh and ahh at her techniques.

She's also probably wonderful at wrapping Christmas presents, a task that Hannah usually loves to do but hasn't had the energy to take on yet. Honey has perfectly wrapped gifts with coordinating paper, large puffy gold bows and calligraphy-written gift tags, all tucked under the tree. Hannah's gifts, what little she's bought, are shoved in an Amazon box in the corner of her closet.

They did get a tree. At first, Derek said he didn't want to put up the tree that Hannah had for years, the one they stored in a giant yellow plastic bin and pulled up from the building's basement storage space every year to put together. He said it reminded him too much of what happened, of the fights they'd had right there in the living room under the glow of those lights, of the "First Christmas Together" ceramic heart ornament that he'd flung across the room to break in a million pieces behind the couch.

Hannah could pull the couch away from the wall right now and find one of those shards, even though she'd vacuumed behind there a dozen times since then. She imagines them beneath her as she sits, counting stitches. It gives her a sick feeling, so she tries to stop, tries to concentrate instead on what she's making. They'd gotten a real tree instead. Derek said he always liked real trees better.

The first set of booties are mismatched—one much bigger than the other. Her second attempt isn't much better, and by the third she is ready to start stabbing people. She holds up the bootie, a lopsided whale with a pointed snout. Carries it into the kitchen, where Derek is making dinner.

"How's this?" she asks him, standing in the doorway.

He barely looks up. He is rummaging through the utensil drawer. Things clatter. "Did you put the grater in here?"

"Yes, yesterday when I unloaded the dishes."

"It's not in here."

"It should be."

He turns. "Well, it's not. Are you sure you put it back in the right place?"

She feels herself getting hot. "Um, yeah."

"Because sometimes you put stuff in weird places."

"I put it back." She pushes past him. She moves the slotted spoons aside and slams it on the counter. "Right here. Just like I said."

"Well, you don't have to get all angry about it. I was just asking."

She stares at him. "Is this how it's always going to be?"

He starts grating cheese into a neat pile on the plate like shedding skin. "What do you mean?"

"I feel like you would be happier if I just left."

He looks up at that. "Don't be ridiculous."

"Maybe you would. I could just get out of here, leave you to be happy on your own."

"Hannah, I couldn't find the grater. No need to go nuclear."

She shakes her head. "I mean, just do it. Get even. Do something. Stab me in the neck. Anything. Just stop this." She feels her tears well up, and that makes her even angrier. Derek steps toward her, but she backs away, shaking her head.

"I don't hate you," he says.

"Then what? What is it? And when does it stop?" Hannah feels like a bird is trapped in her chest, fluttering to find a way out. "I—how long do I have to pay for it?"

The phone rings. She and Derek stand on either side of the kitchen as if someone has taken a snapshot of them, forever frozen in this moment. Then Hannah breaks it, moves.

"Mrs. Tenner, it's Mathilda Bcc. I have a nice place to show you."

"Oh?" Hannah says, her heart still racing. She looks over at Derek, who is staring at her, mouthing something.

"It's a townhouse, but it's in a brand new development. End of the year deals." Honey's voice is so upbeat, so excited. She is expecting the same excitement in return, Hannah knows.

"That's great," Hannah says.

"What?" Derek is asking. His eyes are wide. He comes closer, and Hannah wants to push him back, make him fall into the open drawer. To hear the clatter.

"We'll definitely take a look," Hannah says.

"Who is it?" Derek asks. "What?"

But Hannah just stares at him.

***

His therapist is chewing on the edge of her pen and all Derek can think about is the way his penis looked floating in that hotel bathtub, all wrinkled and defeated and bobbing.

His therapist chuckles, bringing Derek out of the moment. "What?" he asks, suddenly self-conscious.

She shakes her head. "Nothing, nothing. I'm sorry. I was just— well, my dad always joked that even Joseph and Mary would pass up the Days Inn on Main Street. You know, when they were looking for a place to stay? Never mind. Anyway, carry on."

He is telling her again about the separation last year. He's been over this story several times, but she likes to go back. He's stopped trying to figure out why.

"Well, yeah, so it's not the nicest place," he says, still annoyed. He can remember the smell of Room 404, gym locker and bleach. And he never liked the looks of the door lock, which he was pretty sure he could take out with one swipe of a crowbar. The bathtub was too small for him to stretch out his legs, but that didn't stop him from filling it to the top and sitting in his own filth until the water went cold and his fingertips looked like pale raisins.

One night after a particularly hard binge of drinking and feeling sorry for himself, he remembered something his Aunt Bernice had told him about the windows in hotel rooms never opening. *They don't want crazy people committing suicide on their property*, she said. *The lawsuits! Can you imagine?*

The window suicide story nagged at him, and so finally Derek got out of bed and went to check for himself. Pulled back the blackout curtains. To his surprise, and as if to prove Aunt Bernie wrong, there was a little latch on the window that clearly, if lifted, would allow the window to swing open.

It could hardly be called a balcony, but there was just enough room to step out into the ledge and look down onto festive Main Street. "Why hello Santa," Derek said, saluting the plastic figure that posed eternally leaning to the side, one arm above his head in a wave, the other stretched out behind him, nearly scraping Derek's balcony as if trying to hold on. The air rushed in and kicked on the groaning heating unit just below the window. The cold seeped into Derek's socks like water. Below, the rush of holiday traffic and other folks busy with gift-buying for people that didn't betray them. He was wearing gym shorts and a white t-shirt and the December air was hurting the skin around his nipples. But it felt good, too, like a punch in the face slicing through the drunken fog. Fuck Aunt Bernie. What the hell did she know?

And yet, the balcony was not nearly high enough for any man considering ending his life. If anything, you'd get maybe a broken leg or two. Maybe snag an arm on one of the other balconies going down, but chances are you'd just land on the sidewalk below and ruin someone's eggnog and cookies at the café across the street.

"And how did you feel standing there thinking about jumping?"

The therapist's voice comes through like a splash of cold water. Derek blinks, looks over at her. *How do you think I felt, dimwit?* he wants to say, but he doesn't. He is trying to be better.

"I wasn't ever really going to jump," he says, possibly trying to convince both of them. He is pretty sure this is true.

"Mmm," she says, jotting something down in her notebook.

"I just wanted to do something...bad."

The plastic Santa had a fake fucking jolly smile painted on his fat face. He was tied up there by some heavy-duty wire. Derek leaned out far and smacked Santa in the face. Its plastic body swung around a bit, but Santa didn't stop smiling. He punched it this time. It made him laugh, beating up Santa. Then he grabbed hold of the arm that was reaching back and pulled.

It didn't take much. The Santa was old. The arm was only connected by some wires, old wires that no longer worked. There were probably people in the town who still remembered when the big Santa on Main Street waved to them as they walked by with their parents. The Santa hadn't waved in a long time, though. And now he never would again, since his left arm was now propped up against the open window of Room 404.

"Screw you, Santa." He was drunk, he knew, and he also knew this was not his finest moment.

He dragged Santa's arm back into the room. The thing looked kind of trippy under the flickering light of *Inside Edition* flashing, muted, on the TV. Now what? He had to hide the arm. He couldn't very well leave it there for the cleaning crew to find.

He lifted the mattress on the bed. He put the arm there and dropped the mattress, and no, it was clear there was something under there. "Fuck."

Then he saw the long dresser drawers at the bottom of the chest on the other side of the bed. Perfect length for an arm, and who ever looked in those? He slid one open and dropped the arm in there. The arm coffin. Derek stepped back and smiled at his work. He felt strangely satisfied.

"I never use those drawers," his therapist says.

"Exactly," Derek says.

***

Hannah waits outside her office for Honey to pick her up. The snow from the morning has already melted, and piles of black mush clog the curbs. Across the street in front of the grocery store stands the Salvation Army man, ringing his bell. Hannah watches, but no one tosses any money in his bucket.

They are meeting Derek at the townhouse. It is close to his office—a perk Hannah tries to slide into conversations with him—but she knows he will still find something wrong. She knows that forever and ever, no matter how perfect or upbeat or kind she is, he will always find something wrong. It is his right, his privilege, now that she messed up.

The blind lady is coming, that white stick sloshing through the slush piles. She walks slowly. People move around her. She is wearing thick sturdy boots, but Hannah worries. What if there's a patch of ice?

Is the blind lady lonely? Does she live by herself? Hannah imagines all the mundane life chores that would be so difficult—grocery shopping, getting dressed, ordering a drink at a bar. Hannah closes her eyes, searches through the blackness, but all that appears is a faint silhouette of Paul hovering over her, leaning down to kiss her, and she shakes her head, opens her eyes again, grateful for the distractions.

The blind woman approaches the curb, no signs of stopping. Then Honey's car appears, her turn signal blinking. Honey doesn't see the blind lady, or doesn't want to wait, and makes a quick turn to the right, pulling up to the curb beside Hannah. Just as Hannah starts walking toward the car, a man in a gray business suit comes up behind the blind lady.

Honey is waving through the windshield, a beaming smile on her face. Hannah hears the man say, "Sandy! So nice to see you again. Would you like to walk with me?" Hannah opens Honey's door, sinks into the seat just as she sees the man link his arm in the blind lady's arm, just as she hears her say, "Yes, that would be lovely, Tom."

***

The townhouse is bigger than Hannah imagined. It is in a neighborhood of brand-new units, never lived in before. She runs her hand across the shiny granite kitchen counters. It is spacious, modern. There's a sparkling tiled floor. She is secretly happy it's not a dump. Even so, Derek can't help but find something. "Don't be fooled by all the sparkle," he mutters. "These walls are thin. The carpet is cheap."

She ignores him. Hannah starts to see herself there. She likes the little alcove off the living room and the gas fireplace in the den. Built-in bookcases above where the TV could hang. A huge master bedroom with walk-in closet and a gigantic sunken tub ("Imagine having to clean that thing," Derek says). Two smaller bedrooms, one with great light for a nursery. A finished basement with a patio out back. They could have a grill!

"It's a really great price for this area," Honey says. "Good floor plan, good living space. And the parking is pretty generous for a townhouse community."

"Are they having trouble selling these units?" Derek asks as he stares out the patio doors off the kitchen, hands in his pockets. "I see there are a few cars parked in driveways over there, but most of these homes are still on the market, right?"

Shut up, Hannah thinks, and imagines pushing him off the balcony, smiling at his surprised "O" face as he falls.

"They are brand-new," Honey says. "Just on the market a few months ago, really, and already ten units have been sold."

"Well, I love the space," Hannah says. "And we wouldn't have a yard to maintain, Derek. You don't love cutting grass, do you?"

***

His first reaction is to hate it. His second reaction is to hate it more when it's actually a good place. He recognizes it's a good deal. A good neighborhood. Close to his work. He recognizes all of this, and yet.

When did he turn into a person who is spiteful for the sake of being spiteful? It scares him. He watches Mathilda and Hannah wander around the place, oohing and ahhing, and it makes him want to puke. He imagines himself and Hannah sitting in Mathilda's office back in Salmonville, signing the papers, writing away their savings for this place. He feels trapped, like a wild animal caged in a prison of drywall.

But this is what you wanted, a voice says in his ear.

Derek closes his eyes, tries to shut out the panic. It is as though he has several demon monsters swirling inside his stomach, dropping heavy things. He counts to ten, slowly, another trick his therapist taught him. On ten, he opens his eyes again, tries to think of something nice about Hannah. She's taken up crafting, he thinks. She sings lullabies to her stomach when she thinks he isn't listening.

Hannah turns and looks at him. He watches her smile fade. "What do you think?" she asks, and already he sees her preparing for the disappointment.

"It could work," he says, shrugging.

"Really?" The word is a gush, like a blocked faucet suddenly freed. "Oh wow!" She hugs him, almost knocking him over. He finds himself laughing then, and stops, pulls away.

"I mean, we'll have to think about it," he says to Mathilda, but already he knows what's going to happen. Already he can see Mathilda's sly wink at Hannah, her unspoken, *See? We've got him hooked.* He squeezes Hannah's shoulders, pulls her close. "We'll see what happens," he says, but already the dark monsters are rushing upwards again, loading their bricks one by one back into his stomach.

***

"My pervie Uncle Ryan used to own a townhouse, Derek. That's what I think of when I think of townhouses."

Mindy has made herself at home in Derek's office, legs crossed, leaning back in his guest chair and cracking her gum. Derek tries to imagine the apartment Mindy lives in. He pictures it small with cheap furniture, posters of obscure bands tacked on the wall. He has no idea if she lives alone. He has no idea what she does besides watch scary movies.

"It's brand new. And cheaper than a single family." He's annoyed to be defending this to Mindy.

"Brand new? Single family?" Mindy laughs. "Look at you, all family man again. Next you'll be lecturing me on 401(k)s."

"I can't really talk about this anymore," he says, getting up. "I've got a meeting." His knees crack. He's pissed off. Feels old, stupid. Out of touch. Mindy has that way about her—either making him feel young and stupid or old and stupid. He kind of hates her for it.

Mindy laughs again, but it's shorter this time. "Don't get mad, Derek. I'm just joking with you."

But he's already out the door, flicking the switch as he walks, leaving her in the dark.

***

"You did it. Congratulations. You two are proud homeowners!"

Honey's voice is loud enough over the phone that Hannah can hear her even from across the room. Derek is holding the phone a few inches from his ear and nodding, pacing back and forth while Honey gives him the details. Hannah's heart is pounding in her chest. She immediately feels a sharp pang of regret, fear.

When he hangs up, Derek runs his hands through his hair. "Well, there you go," he says. "We got it."

"I can't believe they accepted it so fast," Hannah says.

"Are you not happy about it?"

She shrugs. "I mean, yeah. But it's scary, right? Now that it happened. It's scary. What if we made the wrong decision?"

"Well, it's too late now," he says, and Hannah immediately feels herself getting angry.

"I'm not saying we made the wrong decision. I'm just saying—I'm just saying you never know."

Derek sits in the chair across from her. He stares out the window. They watch a man and his dog pass by. "Yeah. You never know."

They will live there, year after year. A baby—their baby—will run up and down the stairs. She can see a little patch of thinning hair at the top of Derek's head—the part he always rubs—and she imagines him older, bald. Both of them old, always sniping at each other. Their legs long, growing roots through the floor of the new townhouse, tangling around each other deep in the ground, impossible to remove.

This is what she wonders: what if she'd never been caught? Would she have stopped the affair or left Derek? It is a question Derek has never asked her, and she doesn't know how she would answer.

"Well," Derek says, tapping his fingers on the table. "I guess we should celebrate."

He pours some sparkling grape juice into the flutes they got as a wedding present.

"To us," she says, and blushes.

Derek clinks her glass. "To a new start," he says. Hannah feels the bubbles dancing their way down her throat and tries not to cough. She's thinking about the blind lady again, how this morning on her way to work Hannah saw her walking off-path, wandering toward one of the pillars under the entrance to the bank, trying to feel her way around it with the stick. Hannah wonders how often that happens—how many times she's strayed off her route, and how she ends up finding her way back.

***

As they get closer and closer to Christmas, Derek's therapist get fixated on questions about Derek's childhood holidays. "Did your parents celebrate Christmas? Did you believe in Santa? How did you feel when you found out he wasn't real?"

"I was pissed off for awhile, I guess, but like everyone else I kind of started to suspect. My father wouldn't even bother to change his own handwriting on the gift tags. And we never had a chimney."

The therapist is also interested in the baby. She wants to know how Derek feels about that. "Will you tell your own child about Santa Claus?"

"Hell no," Derek says at first. It is a gut reaction. But of course... "I don't know. I don't want to, but I don't want him—or her—to be a freak."

"Do you trust Hannah?" the therapist asks. He knows what she's getting at—does Derek believe he's the father—but he won't go there.

"I guess so." He feels like they skipped seven steps in this process. He feels like, with all this jolly old St. Nick and presents under the tree crap, he's regressed backwards, picked off the scab, and started bleeding again.

"It sounds like you're still grappling with her betrayal, still punishing her."

He felt his anger flare up. She's the one who did this to them. Derek didn't go banging someone all over town. He didn't betray their vows, make their marriage into a joke. But he pushes past it. He knows the therapist will jump all over that. This is what he's supposed to be working on. "It's the time of the year," he says. "I just—I hate the holidays."

"Do you think you are mentally prepared to be a father?"

He wonders how many hours he spent in that hotel bed thinking about Hannah and the scumbag, wondering if she ever texted Derek while she had the guy's dick in her other hand. If she ate French fries off his stomach. It kills him, too, that in spite of all that, he wishes he'd never found out about it. It pisses him off that she was so sloppy. She never was good with the details, always messing up the edges of paint jobs, spilling wine on her collar, forwarding emails she shouldn't.

"You know, remember how you told me to try to walk in Hannah's shoes for awhile? To see her side of things? Maybe that's exactly what I need to do." He smiles at the therapist, feeling his lips curl over his teeth. "Maybe I need to sleep with someone else, see how it feels."

She is unfazed, and Derek finds himself a bit disappointed. He realizes how much he wanted to shock her. "You could try that," she says, "but think about how that will make you feel."

Derek is done for the day. His head hurts. The sun streams in the window like a laser beam. "I know exactly how that will make me feel," he says.

***

On the Wednesday before Christmas, Derek leaves work a little early to catch the downtown theater's early showing of the classic *Black Christmas*. Hannah is working the late shift, so he buys a big box of Goobers and some nachos and calls that dinner. He settles down in his seat, stretches out his legs, and just starts to make a dent in the cold container of cheese when he hears his name. He looks up in surprise and sees Mindy—of course—standing in the aisle, looking up at him. A woman with tattoos leaking from under her short-sleeved black t-shirt stands behind her sipping a very large soda.

"Hey," he says. "Fancy seeing you here."

Mindy shakes her head. "You didn't tell me..." she trails off, looks back at her friend, then pushes her way past Derek to the empty seats beside him. Derek moves his Goobers and his coat to his lap.

Her friend's name is Martina, and she's got some weird large disc in her earlobe that Derek is afraid to look at too closely. The movie starts and he is pleased to not have to make small talk.

It is an odd movie, slowly paced and nonsensical in places, and Mindy's friend Martina talks in loud whispers over the boring parts. When it is over, the three of them congregate in the lobby, discussing the movie, which Martina did not like very much. "You don't even like scary movies, silly," Mindy tells her, tapping Martina's cheek with her finger, and Derek wonders if they are on a date. "No wonder you didn't get it."

Martina pulls out her phone, and starts flipping through her email. Mindy turns away from her and looks at Derek. She says, "Well, who wants to go for drinks?" Derek is about to beg off when Martina looks up and shakes her head. "I'm beat. I've gotta run."

Mindy looks like someone just stole her puppy, but then she blinks and straightens up. "Looks like it's just you and me then," she tells him, and he doesn't know how to say no.

***

Mindy likes sweet drinks with lots of fruit. She downs three while they eat some combo appetizer platter with different colored dips and various deep fried foods piled on one another.

"So who's Martina?" he asks.

She looks up at him, shoves a jalapeño popper in her mouth. She rolls her eyes, chews, swallows. "A lost cause."

"Oh yeah?"

She shrugs. "She's not into me because I'm bi."

"That's too bad."

Mindy winks, leans in. "Maybe she was jealous of you."

He lets that one roll off him. He realizes he could sleep with her tonight if he wanted to. It is as obvious as if she handed it to him all wrapped up in a neat little present. *Here you go*, her smile says. Her leg bumps into his under the table, and he shifts in his booth, not sure where to put himself.

"Do you need some water?" he asks. Derek wonders what would happen if someone they knew walked in—Hannah's friend Frances, or a neighbor. He thinks about the Days Inn, just a few blocks down the road. He knows the route so well. It would be so easy.

Mindy wants to talk, that's clear. She complains about her boss; Derek has heard it before. She finds him creepy. "Dude's like eighty years old and he's looking at my cleavage."

"He's not eighty, Mindy. More like sixties."

"Whatever." She waves him off. Takes a sip of her green drink. Looks him in the eye. "Everyone's the same, you know. We're all assholes. It's okay."

"Yeah," he says. "I guess so."

"I really hate Christmas," she says with a snort, but he can see as she looks away that there is sadness there. "Everyone acts all nice to each other for a few days, and then they go back to being selfish fucks. It's nauseating."

He tries to picture Mindy around a dinner table with family. He feels a wave of nostalgia then, a tenderness for this whole stupid notion of Christmas, and wants to prove her wrong. He wants the whole gamut— trees and presents and eggnog. He wants to be away from the generic noise of this restaurant and walking around in the snow singing carols. He just wants comfort, love, in whatever form. It is such an intense feeling that when the waitress comes by, Derek asks for the check without consulting Mindy. He looks her in the eye, urgent. Already in his mind he is several steps ahead in the evening, unraveling the plan.

"Do you want to go to the Days Inn with me?" he asks.

***

The snow everyone's been talking about starts early, scaring away the last of Hannah's clients. She turns up the heat in the apartment and eats a quick dinner of leftover spaghetti.

She should get some things in order—pack books they could give away to a charity, or throw away some junk. They have accumulated so much.

Instead, she does laundry. She loves folding towels and sheets, making them into perfect little squares, all lined the same way. She loves that they all fit perfectly in the linen closet in stacks of four.

She checks her phone. No message from Derek. She wanders into the kitchen, peels an orange. She eats it standing at the window, watching the snow fall faster now. They are expecting up to five inches. The newscasters keep making puns about having a white Christmas.

While she's watching, Honey Bee's little black Toyota pulls up in front of the building, blocking three other cars in. The real estate agent gets out, a scarf wrapped around her hair, and drags out her big bag. A few minutes later the doorbell rings.

The list of New Year's resolutions Honey must make every year! And she probably keeps every one of them. Hannah smiles at Honey as she opens the door, but she realizes how defeated Honey always makes her feel. *Bake one new kind of cake each month! Exercise thirty minutes every day! Write handwritten letters to people on their birthdays!*

"Hannah, my dear," she says, walking inside without an invitation. She is fumbling with her bag. "I just wanted to get you this paperwork before the snow. I told Derek I was dropping it off—did he tell you?"

"You shouldn't have come out in this weather."

"Oh, snow, schmow," Honey says, waving a fat, manicured hand. "I grew up in Shawano, Wisconsin. This was summer for us." She laughs like a large shotgun going off, and hands Hannah a thick folder. "Just look this over for the closing."

When Honey's cell rings, Hannah is not surprised to hear the sound of a little bell ringing, like the sound you hear when you open an old gift shop's door. "Excuse me," she says, and turns her back, facing the door. Hannah can hear a man's voice on the other end, perhaps a boy, definitely male. And then Honey, loudly, "There's Hamburger Helper in the cabinet." Pause. "Yes, you can." Pause. "It's in the cabinet with all the other pots and pans." She looks over at Hannah, shakes her head. "I don't know. I don't know. Maybe 6:30. Maybe later." Pause. "Okay. No. Okay. I've got to go. Okay. Bye."

"I swear," she says, fumbling with her phone. "I swear, Hannah, they are going to be the death of me one of these days. Do they think I have time to cook?"

Hannah blinks. She has never used Hamburger Helper in her life. It is no better than dog food, her mom used to say.

"Anyway, just look that over and let me know if you have any questions. I'll be in the office all day tomorrow. We're closed Christmas, you know, but other than that I'm around." Honey leaves as quickly as she came, and Hannah is left with sudden quiet and the hint of her strong rose perfume.

Hannah shoves the orange peels down the garbage disposal. She likes the violent sound it makes as it tears them up. She doesn't open the folder. The paperwork is too intimidating—this she will leave for Derek. She turns the heat up again. She will miss how quickly the place heats up, that comforting smell of the radiator.

The wind kicks up and outside the snow is dancing in circles. Already her car has a light dusting, and she realizes she forgot to lift up the windshield wipers like Derek always tells her to. He loves shoveling snow. He's already brought out the bag of road salt and set it next to the front door. Even though there are days that he doesn't really talk to her, he always gets up and cleans off her car. It's how she knows it's still okay.

***

It was there.

The room was just how he remembered it, small, suffocating. Mindy had stayed off to the side, careful not to touch the sticky remote control on the desk, the cheap pad of stationary, the plastic cup. She hadn't really believed him when he told her what he was looking for, but the big dresser was still there, too, and after he pulled the arm out and waved it at her, she had to believe. She just shook her head. "You're goddamn nuts."

He may be goddamn nuts, but he is also excited, pumped on adrenaline. Finally, something feels right. After dropping Mindy off at the bus stop—"Just don't get arrested, because you'll have a hell of a lot of explaining to do with that in the back seat"—he drives home, singing loudly along to "O Holy Night" on the radio. It's a classic version by Frank Sinatra or Bing Crosby or one of those guys, the deep, strong voice providing comfort and a sense of nostalgia.

The Santa arm spans the back seat of his car, chubby and pink, with the wires still hanging off the end. He can hardly believe his luck. He wants to show it to Hannah, even though he knows she isn't going to understand. He wants to one day explain to his child that this is a special object. He wishes it wasn't an arm. He wishes it was a pretty gemstone or a rare penny or even a heavy vase. He feels like the father in *A Christmas Story* who wins the leg lamp; only he can see the beauty of it.

The snow is falling fast, but it isn't sticking to the road. Still, it has scared most everyone inside and for the most part Derek is alone. Soon there will be a new route home. He won't be needing this key much longer, and the parking space assigned to him in front of their building will be someone else's spot, someone else's home. He feels very old. He feels very tired. But he feels good.

As he pulls up to his building, he sees Hannah framed in the window, standing by the sink cleaning up the rest of the dishes. He remembers one of their first Christmases together—a year they decided to disappoint both sides of the family and spend the holiday alone together. They made hot dogs and s'mores and made love next to the fire, the room lit only by the tree lights. How much he had loved her then. How happy they'd been.

He is struck by all that has happened, but not in a fresh deep cut kind of way, but more like a soldier whose battle wounds have healed and made him stronger. His therapist would be proud of him. And so, he thinks, the Santa arm is more like a peace offering—a chubby plastic olive branch. It is with this that he walks down the sidewalk, presses the elevator button, and uses the key to open what will soon be someone else's house. It is with this that he waits for Hannah to turn, to smile, to see everything that is ahead of them and all that is behind them.

Entrapment

There was something about ruining someone else's career that really motivated me to get out of bed. That sounds negative, I know, but I've never been much of a morning person. Most days at 7:34 a.m.—even with The Professor, my iguana, digging his claws into my naked back—I'd say screw that and roll back over, slapping my hand on top of the alarm clock. But that morning was a special day.

"All right, Prof," I groaned, my mouth feeling as dry as his scales. "I'm up."

I'm Paul, by the way. Paul Reston. That's the name my parents crowned me with when I popped out of the womb and started howling. However, you might know me by my other name: Harrison Teeth. I know, the last name is a little pretentious and sounds made-up—that's what people say. They have no idea that Paul Reston, movie critic and restaurant reviewer for the *Daily Star*, is also Harrison Teeth, investigative reporter.

So Harrison Teeth or Paul Reston, or whoever I was at that god awful hour of the morning, shoved on some dirty jeans, carried The Professor back to his domain, and unlocked the dead bolt to find the paper. My new apartment building, which I moved into about seven months ago when Mary Beth left me, had an early bird newspaper carrier. When Mary Beth and I lived uptown our carrier was a grouchy old man who delivered the paper sometime between 10:00 and 11:00 a.m. So that was one of the positives of my new apartment complex—add it to the (meager) list. An almost-working security system that allowed me to beep in guests from downstairs, an extra bedroom for The Professor to roam around in, and a location on the other side of the building from the garbage dumpsters, so the smell of decay and shit only occasionally wafted over.

No balcony, no yard, and Mary Beth got to keep the dog and the kid (most of the time), but I was trying to keep it upbeat.

The paper was there, faithful as ever, a single pink rubber band holding it in a tight roll. *The Daily Star* in fancy scroll script. My story above the fold, front page. I could see the top of the Judge's head, just peeking out below the masthead. His giant, might-as-well-be-a-mugshot image was arriving on 120,000 doorsteps all across this fine city. There was a certain power in knowing I was responsible for feeding many people their water cooler chatter as the sun rose in the blue sky that morning.

"Hi, Mr. Paul!"

In my reverie, I hadn't heard Theresa approaching. I suppressed a groan, looking up to see her ambling toward me. About that time, my head started pounding, remembering that I was dehydrated from the ten or so beers I had the night before after my editor finally put the story through.

"Can I come in quick and see The Professor?"

I knew that's what she was going to say, broken record that she was. Unshaven, still half-asleep, I wanted to be mean, but there was the guilt. Watch it, watch it, here it comes. Yep. Swelling up inside of me. She was fifteen or sixteen years old, but she looked about twelve. She had some kind of growth deficiency for Christ's sake. She always had this acidic smell about her, like she just came from the hospital, and her arms pushed out of her baggy t-shirts like twigs from a pathetic Christmas tree.

"Hey, Theresa, well, it's probably not a real good time right now—" The truth was that it was a good time because iguanas are happiest in the mornings.

"Just for a few minutes," she said in that familiar whining voice. It grated on me, but it was damn hard to say no. "Before I have to go to school." If I was Theresa's guidance counselor, I'd tell her to go into sales.

I looked down at the paper, feeling my impatience grow. It was there, screaming to be read. I wanted to see if Tim had cut the fourth graf after all, if he'd included Lila's picture of the scene of the arrest.

Theresa shuffled her feet, not meeting my eyes. There would be no way for her to know I had a pet iguana except for the fact that she and her mom saw me in the hall one afternoon as I was juggling my keys and several large tree branches I'd filched from the woodsy area behind the buildings. It looked strange, sure. Anyone would've asked what I was doing.

"I'm kind of getting ready..." I trailed off, knowing it was futile. She pushed past, muttering something about not being long. I took one wishful glance down the end of the hallway, hoping to see her mother poke her head around and call the kid back, but no such luck. It was my own fault, anyway. After Theresa took such interest in The Professor, I sort of had a soft spot for her and her mother. It was good to know people in the building. Just in case. You never knew when you might need a cup of milk or a charged cell phone.

Theresa went right for the back room, the Professor's room, and opened the door. It was hot in there, and I could feel the screen of heat pass over my face as I followed her in, watching tentatively from the doorway. The Professor had moved back to his favorite spot, basking under the heat lamp, his green scales magnificent in the light. I was struck, like always, at just how odd he looked—an ancient, wrinkled dinosaur from the distant past.

"Hi, monster," Theresa breathed at him. The Professor sneezed, but otherwise gave no indication we'd barged into his pad. "When does he sleep?" she asked.

"Most of the time."

"Does he eat everything?" she asked. She always had weird questions, as if asking just one more meant she could stay longer to wait for the answer.

"No, just lots of vegetables." That was the beauty of the iguana— he's an herbivore, so no live insects for The Professor. He eats rhubarb, lettuce, spinach, beets, radishes, turnips, and occasionally, when I'm feeling generous, pizza. The Professor loves nothing more than to climb the tree branch I've propped up behind my La-Z-Boy and chow down on some Papa John's pizza crust.

"Why does he like the light so much?" Theresa's nervous tic was out now—sniffling and squeezing her nose with her fingers. I have a special talent for searching out nervous tics in other people. It helps me figure out if I am winning in certain situations, or if I stand a chance at all. If I can't find the tic in someone, then they bring out *my* nervous tic.

"Helps him digest his food," I said and immediately regretted it because I could already imagine the barrage of questions that came along with that answer. *What do you mean? Why would the light help that? How does he poop? Where does he poop? Can I stay here forever and be your best friend and never stop asking you questions, never ever ever for as long as we both live?*

I snuck a look down at the paper, peeled off the rubber band, and fitted it around my wrist. The matter-of-fact headline blared out, "Judge Charged in Child Sex Sting." Then my byline, "By Harrison Teeth, *Daily Star* Investigative Reporter." I felt the itch under my skin. Anticipation. I always got it when I saw my story in print.

I never wanted to be a journalist. I wanted to be a cop. I enrolled in the academy, and after the first few weeks realized it wasn't for me. The other cadets were dumb, sexist, racist blockheads. I couldn't see spending the rest of my career driving a squad car around with a guy whose idea of a good time is shooting beer cans off a burned tree stump. I need to feel smart, surround myself with smart people. I think that's why I named the iguana The Professor, the smartest one on *Gilligan's Island* (I prefer to think of my reference to that awful TV show as ironic, not an indication of some hypocrisy on my part).

I was always a pretty good writer, so I thought doing the cops beat at a daily might be the second best thing. One thing led to another, and I found myself heading up the ranks at the paper, getting more and more stories, sources calling at odd hours. Mary Beth was frightened of the people calling the house, shady characters for sure, and she told me that I couldn't use my real name if I was publishing these kind of things, that these people might hunt us down and burn crosses in our yard or kidnap our daughter, or worse—ruin her reputation in the neighborhood.

So I reluctantly agreed to an alias.

At first I thought it would be a let-down. Work hundreds of hours busting your ass to uncover a story and then not even see your name in print. But then it ended up being kind of fun, working under another name. Having another identity. A secret identity.

That, and I sort-of started to think of Harrison Teeth as my other self, a whole separate person with separate rules. Not in a weird split-personality way. More like in the way it is when you get really drunk and you start to see yourself as invincible, witty, engaging, and really attractive. Harrison Teeth seemed like that kind of guy. Very good on the page, very good on the street. The kind of guy you want to talk to at a cocktail party.

* * *

By the time I got Theresa out of my apartment and had fully savored my story over black, black coffee, most of the morning traffic had died down. The newsroom was buzzing, however. I made my way to my desk and sat down. Blinking light on the Harrison Teeth phone. Nineteen messages already. The red light blinking extra fast to let me know my voice mail was full. The Paul Reston phone was sadly, humbly silent.

Before I had a chance to check messages, Lila snaked her white miniskirt way across the room and propped herself on the corner of my desk, tapping a folder in my direction. "You, my friend, are the most popular guy in town today."

"Not Paul Reston."

Lila shook her head. "Mr. Teeth."

"Ah, Mr. Teeth. Popular? Or notorious?"

"Aren't those one and the same?" Lila and I often ended up working together on assignments. She was fresh out of college but with a driven attitude that you didn't see as much in the younger generation. Don't get me wrong—she was still a bit wild. She was the only photographer on staff who regularly came to the office dressed like she worked on Wall Street, but then shared the intimate details of her piercings and drank the boys under the table at happy hour. But she did good work. The fact that she had gotten roped into some of the aftermath of my divorce proceedings and yet still didn't hate me over it was something to admire as well.

"It appears, Mr. Teeth, that your story has some bite to it. The Judge is not happy."

"Neither is The Professor," I muttered under my breath.

"What?" she asked.

"Nothing. Have we been getting calls?"

"Calls?" Lila laughed. "Mr. Teeth, this is way beyond calls."

"What do you mean?"

"You must not have been watching television. The Judge has been on every morning news show. Saying that the police acted illegally—I think the word 'entrapment' was tossed around a lot with the lawyer types. That Harrison Teeth was on a personal mission to destroy his character. That my pictures were illegal. Oh, it's ugly."

"Good thing I'm just little old Paul Reston, reviewer of movies and dinner theater plays."

Lila smiled, clucking her tongue in that way she did. Her tic—though it wasn't a nervous one. It was more of a sign of contentment, that she'd just won. A sly cat purring in the sun, was what that tic was. I don't even think she realized she did it.

"We're having a staff meeting in five. Roberts was waiting until you got in." She brushed her short black hair from her face and put the folder down on my desk. She lifted her arms above her head, stretching, revealing a spiked leather bracelet beneath her sleeve. Even in her dress shirt and miniskirt, there was something about Lila that was a bit punk.

"Jesus, couldn't you have given me some notice?"

"Well, if you had a smart phone like everyone else on the planet, maybe I could."

I rolled my eyes. Here's when the age difference got in the way—she didn't understand how someone might not want a device that could track your whereabouts at all times. Hell, when I told her where The Professor's name had come from, she'd never heard of *Gilligan's Island*. Talk about making a guy feel old.

"Well, I came to tell you about the meeting, but I was also hoping I could take you to lunch today to celebrate," she said, picking up the folder.

I cringed, remembering Mary Beth. "Oh shit, Lila, I can't. I have to meet Mary Beth. Stuff about Megan. She's having trouble in school."

"Oh, well, that's fine. Another time."

"Maybe dinner after work next week," I said.

"Maybe." She avoided my eyes. I knew she was thinking about what my wife had accused her of. Even though it had cooled down lately, it was still a sore spot.

Awkward pause broken by one of the graphic designers, Tim. "Hey Jackass," he called me, his term of endearment. "Staff meeting in the conference room. Everyone wants a piece of you." Then he turned to Lila. "Looking fine."

Lila blew him a kiss. He responded by squeezing her ass. Politically correct we are not.

***

Lunch. I met Mary Beth at her favorite café in downtown. We'd gone there once on a date, one of the first. We were different people then, happy, free, not the two bitter souls sitting across from one another at a rickety metal table, snacking on pretzels and hot mustard sauce and calculating the other's next move.

These meetings were dangerous. That's what my lawyer told me. He said that if I tried to play nice, I was going to get burned. I still have a hard time believing it. For one thing, Mary Beth no longer brought up Lila's name. I saw that as a victory. We talked strictly business (the kid), but there was no hair-pulling, no name-calling (usually). There were no inside jokes, either. All that history between us, just fallen away. It was sad. But we dealt with it. What doesn't kill you...

"I'm worried about Megan," Mary Beth dropped in my lap about halfway through lunch. I wiped the corner of my lip where the mustard was burning a hole.

"What about her now? Grades? Boys?"

"Her teacher says she's being unresponsive."

I laughed. It came out cynical, which is probably the way I intended. I'd always had a problem laughing in inappropriate situations.

Mary Beth ignored it. "She thinks it's because of the divorce. She thinks maybe Megan's not spending enough time with both of us."

"With both of us? That's ridiculous. Doesn't she know what divorce means?" But as I said it, I realized what Mary Beth was really saying, what she didn't want to say, why she was getting all flushed in the face— the counselor was saying that my daughter needed to spend more time with me. Good ole dad.

"Paul, listen, I still stand firm that having Megan with me is the best thing for her," Mary Beth rushed through her words, picking up pieces of salt from the table and grinding them between her finger-nails. "But maybe you could take her a little more. Do things with her, you know? Not just sit around that apartment like you do, with that animal."

A few retorts came to mind: we don't just sit around, The Professor is not just some animal, that I would do more things with my daughter if Mary Beth hadn't been threatening to sue me frontwards and backwards for the past seven months. But I was so elated with her obvious discomfort, with her sudden willingness to put her child's needs in front of her own sense of revenge, that I wanted to jump up and cheer.

As if she read my mind, Mary Beth straightened up in her chair and pulled her jacket tighter around her breasts. She pressed the back of her hand lightly up against her bangs, fluffing them. She wanted lunch to be over.

"I could take her next weekend," I said. "Up to my parents. They can spoil her with presents, feed her poison about my abilities as a parent—though I'm sure she gets enough of that from you—and stuff her with goulash and sausage and whatever else my mom has lying around the house."

"Next weekend is my weekend," she said, the familiar iciness returning. I was used to it by now, but man, in the beginning it had completely thrown me for a loop. All the accusations, especially how untrue and from left field they were, really nailed me to the wall.

"Well, you just said... You have her all week, Mary Beth."

"I know." She paused. "Let me think about it." Perhaps she recognized her iciness as a natural defense around me, something she did even when she didn't need to.

Mary Beth looked troubled, pinching her bottom lip. I leaned over, touched her arm. "Hey. It'll be okay. She's a good kid."

She pulled away from my touch, but not unkindly. "I know. Right."

The waiter came and dropped the check. Mary Beth picked that time to head for the bathroom. She always had good timing. I opened my wallet to pay the bill, and there was Megan, staring back at me. School picture from a few years ago. She wore a little too much eye make-up, giving her that raccoon look that all the pre-teens had, and she smiled only slightly in order to hide the braces. Rarely did I see that smile anymore, replaced by a constant scowl, or an eye roll. The last time

I'd gotten her to laugh was when I'd cursed profusely at The Professor for leaving a nice pile of shit in my clean laundry basket.

Mary Beth came back just after the waiter took the check. "Thanks for lunch, Paul. I've got to head back to the office now. We'll talk about next weekend, okay?"

And then she was gone, only the trail of her perfume remaining, and I realized that she'd never even mentioned the story or the Judge.

***

The Judge made several mistakes. For one thing, he gained a reputation for being harsh at sentencing. When I, as Harrison Teeth, dug into his records, I found the Judge had a 95 percent conviction rate for sex crimes—rapes, prostitution, child pornography. The district attorney said that the Judge had one time told a defendant that he hoped "God has Mercy on your soul, because I don't."

The Judge prided himself on being a family guy. Married for thirty-seven years to a banker's daughter, with three kids. The Judge's family went to church every Sunday morning for 9:00 a.m. Mass, never fail. All five of them lined up like ducks in one of the pews toward the front of the church, waiting to accept the communion wafer with their tongues.

He was a stand-up guy, they said. Laughed at your jokes, but would never tell a dirty one (at least not in mixed company). Occasionally swirled a brandy with a cigar, but frowned on drinking, especially in excess. Believed in the Bible, America, and our military.

The perfect set-up for destruction.

Every politician has a secret, everybody has a double life that they don't want their friends to find out about. It's what keeps the world ticking. What keeps the papers selling.

It started with an anonymous call to the Harrison Teeth phone line one afternoon at the *Star*. A tip from a source down at the police station hinted that maybe the Internet Crime Division had a big fish to fry. That something was going to go down, that someone who was someone was about to head to a house to meet up with an undercover cop that he thought was a thirteen-year-old girl ready to lose her virginity.

I knew that the ICD had been cracking down hard on online predators, and that if one of the baddies was someone prominent, we had a story. The thought of it was enough to get my heart hammering.

The source tipped me off on the time and place, though he didn't tell me the name of the baddie—just that it was someone political. Lila and I got in a nondescript Honda Accord and parked it in a playground conveniently across the street from the sting house. There we were, Harrison Teeth, investigative reporter, and Lila Santos, ace photographer, dressed the part: Teeth in a grungy t-shirt and jeans, Lila with her short black hair covered by a New York Yankees ball cap. She was cradling her Nikon like a baby.

You couldn't tell anything was going down. It was a quiet neighborhood east of the city, upper middle-class but not too ritzy. The kind of place that wasn't the ghetto, but wasn't too upscale to be threatening for a predator. In fact, with the dim sound of a lawnmower buzzing a few blocks away, the sun shining through the trees, everything calm and soothing, I was sweating a little that maybe the source had been wrong.

But then I saw a jogger trot by holding a hand to one ear and I knew this was it. I felt a twinge of anticipation in my groin and adjusted myself. Harrison Teeth was ready for the story.

After about two hours, a Lincoln Continental drove by slowly. The driver stared at the house, rode past, and in about five minutes passed again from the other side. This happened about five times, and then I saw another car with two men in it, the driver holding a radio. The cops were getting antsy.

The Lincoln Continental finally pulled over to the curb, about five houses down from the sting house. And just sat there.

"He's got cold feet," I muttered to Lila. We both knew it. The fish the cops wanted to fry looked like he was ready to leap out of the pan before they even had a chance to turn up the heat.

And then something strange happened, something that made Lila straighten up in her seat like someone had just twanged her ass with a rubber band. A girl walked out of the sting house. She looked about thirteen—I would've believed it, even though I knew how these things worked and knew she had to be at least eighteen. She was wearing a t-shirt, pink skirt down past her knees, sneakers, and a baseball cap. Her long braid trailed out the back of her hat.

The girl looked around, approaching the car cautiously. Lila sucked air between her teeth. "Seriously?" she whispered. "They're sending her out? Bastards."

The car was still running. I expected that at any moment whoever was inside would take notice of the girl and book it out of there. But he stayed where he was. The girl tapped on the passenger window with her knuckles. She leaned down, gave a little wave. From where we were sitting we could see the toothy grin the girl gave the guy.

"Are you getting this?" I asked Lila, but she was already peering through the lens, deep in concentration.

They talked for awhile. The girl was trying to convince him to come up. She kept pointing at the house. But the driver had chickened out. The girl was desperate now, knowing what her role was supposed to be. I could imagine the conversation playing out. *Well, if you don't want to come up, maybe we could talk a little? Would you like that?*

And then the Judge made the decision that got his mug shot on the doorstep of 120,000 subscribers of the *Daily Star*. He leaned over, popped open the passenger door of his car, and let the girl inside.

"I hope this guy rots in hell," Lila murmured, her face so close to the window her nose was almost touching it.

Swarms of undercover police, as well as screaming squad cars, suddenly descended upon the car as Lila clicked away like she was being

paid by the second. I jotted in my notebook, capturing the scene. A drop
of sweat settled in Harrison Teeth's inner ear. The situation was so good.
He could taste it.

***

Mary Beth had sworn Lila and I were having an affair. It had been her reason
for leaving, though it was really the final excuse for a decision that had long
been brewing. The more I denied it, the more certain she was. Her divorce
lawyer salivated at the thought of proof, but there was none to be found.

At first it was flattering to think that my wife thought a twenty-one-
year old would be interested in me. Then it was a bit of a joke. Then it
wasn't funny anymore.

I'm guessing part of it was that Lila and I spent a lot of time together
doing stories. I'm guessing it was also that Mary Beth wanted a reason,
any reason, to get out of her "big mistake." These are all guesses. For my
little bit of investigative reporting, I'm not much of a detective when it
comes to my own life. That's probably why I didn't see it coming.

I drew the line in the sand when Mary Beth called Lila at her place
in the middle of the night. "What are you doing with my husband?"
she apparently asked, what Lila relayed to me later.

And other things, cuss words, probably some derogatory terms
worthy of the Judge. Lila, to her credit, wouldn't tell me everything. I
admired her for that. Most kids wouldn't have dealt with it as well as
she did. She said she understood where Mary Beth was coming from,
even felt some sympathy for her. "My best friend in college found out
her boyfriend was cheating on her. I saw what she went through," Lila
told me. "I wouldn't wish that on anyone." I didn't have the heart to tell
Lila that some college relationship couldn't possibly compare to an eigh-
teen-year marriage—that seeing your teenage daughter look at you with
hate in her eyes was nothing compared to some tears on a dorm room
pillow. Then again, it's all about perspective.

***

All the news folks hang out at the Chinese restaurant across the street. No one knows the name of the place. We call it Kung Pao Special because the only sign in the window announces the specials of the day in crooked handwriting sketched out on a dingy dry eraser board. It's the quickest and cheapest place for booze.

The bartender on duty Tuesday night was a short, stout guy named Huan. He might have been the owner, but no one was clear on that. He nodded as Lila and I took our places on the squeaky, black velvet bar stools. They all liked us there. When we started popping over after work, they realized we were alcoholics and they could make lots of money if they kept the place open for us to drink. So even though they officially close at 10:00 p.m. most nights, if we're in there before the door locks, they'll let us stay and drink as late as we want. The waiters have been known to start their own mahjongg games or poker tournaments while waiting for us to call it a night. We thought the *Daily Star* probably kept the place afloat. Except for lunchtime, the restaurant had only a smattering of guests and the bar was always empty.

Huan dealt us two Corona coasters. "I'll have a Bird of Paradise tonight," Lila said. She always drank the weird frou-frou drinks on the menu—got a kick out of going down the list: Blue Hawaii, Zombie, Mai Tai, Around the World.

"Guinness," I said.

Kung Pao Special was special in its thoughtful attention to details. Behind the bar was a crooked poster of Marilyn Monroe right next to a wooden statue of an old Chinese man. A massive fish tank separated the restaurant from the bar area. About a half dozen fat goldfish swirled around in there like shiny coins. When I got really drunk, I fantasized about catching them and swallowing them whole.

Lila folded one leg under herself on the barstool and swirled around to face me. "So do you have all your sources in line? Your facts straight?"

She was imitating Roberts from the staff meeting that morning. The thing about Roberts—he pretty much let us go where our instincts took us, but then when the shit hit the fan, he panicked, making sure we'd covered all our bases. As long as we gave him the proof he needed to prevent any law suits, we were his golden children. But if you didn't dot all the "i"'s, watch out.

"I passed on all my notes. Our boss is pacified and has once again retreated back to his cave."

Lila nodded. "I keep dreaming about the Judge," she said.

"What about him?"

"I don't know. He pops up. Randomly. I dreamt I was at a pool party and he was there. The other night, I opened the refrigerator and he was squeezed up inside it, hiding behind the orange juice. Scares the shit out of me."

"He's a creep. Bothers me that Megan's out in the world with these kind of guys."

Lila shivered involuntarily, stared at me. I got the feeling I'd disappointed her somehow. But then she said, "Megan's probably too smart for that crap."

"I hope so."

"What do you mean, you hope so?" She laughed. "You're Harrison Teeth, remember? You know everything."

I wasn't sure if she was making fun of me or not, a usual thing around Lila. The problem with my theory of my secret life guy—the witty, invincible, attractive guy at the cocktail party—is that that guy always wakes up the next morning and winces at all the stuff he did say the night before.

Huan brought us our drinks, my frosted mug of thick, dark beer and Lila's tall, curvy glass filled with an unnaturally blue frozen mess and topped with a chunk of pineapple, a smushed cherry, and a paper umbrella all held together with a pale pink plastic sword.

"Tacky," I said.

"I drink them because they remind me of you."

"Nice." I paused. "Didn't your dad ever teach you how to drink drinks that put hair on your chest?"

She made a sound in her throat. "He never taught me shit. How long have you known me now?"

I shrugged. "A year and a half?"

"And you still don't know that my dad is an off-limits subject?" She said it dramatically, in the kind of tone that people use when they want you to ask them about it, notice it, pay attention to it. I knew that. She'd never said anything specific, but she'd hinted before about it. Something had given her that personal stake in the Judge's story. I didn't like to think about it.

She stared at me, locked her gaze in, and I wondered if she wanted me to ask. But we didn't have that kind of relationship. Behind her eyes was something dark and distant, and it scared me. I looked away.

Then she laughed. Her face brightened artificially and she pulled at the cherry on the sword. "Besides, I am tacky. It's my mission in life."

"Good to have a plan," I said, feeling guilty for letting it go.

The door to the restaurant opened and Tim came in, dragging a draft of cold air with him.

"Early night tonight?" Tim said to Huan, who just nodded his head. Tim situated himself around the corner of the bar, on the other side of Lila. I felt her shut off, whatever it was. He winked at her, nodded at me, and ordered a bourbon from Huan.

"What a fucking night," he said, his tic. Every time he sat down somewhere, he said that. I think even if it was his birthday and he won the lottery and got to swim naked with ten *Playboy* models, he'd still say it. What a fucking night.

"Do a few shots and you'll get over it," Lila said, tracing the edge of the curvy glass with her finger. Now she was leaning closer to Tim, flirting with him. If she had longer hair, she'd be twirling it around her finger. Poor guy didn't even recognize her advances.

"I don't know," Tim said, rubbing his face vigorously with both hands like he was trying to rid himself of memories. "Fucking Hyder's been on my back again about the design guide."

"That's random," Lila said, even though it wasn't. Hyder was the style guide Nazi.

"Yeah, whatever." Tim looked at us both then, as if for the first time. Huan had gone in the back for something, and it was quiet in the place. "Did I interrupt a date or something?"

I snorted. "Now that's random," I said, annoyed.

"I don't know. You two all alone…"

"What's that supposed to mean?" I asked him. This shit was irritating. I'm sure the rumors had been flying around the office for months—people couldn't keep their mouths shut when it came to gossip—but at least he could have some respect in front of us.

Lila just laughed, leaning closer to him, and from what I could see under the bar her knee brushed up against Tim's thigh. If his comments bothered her, she wasn't showing it. "Don't be ridiculous," she said in this strange, girly voice.

"Yeah, you're more her type," I said, hoping to give him a clue.

"What's that mean?" Tim asked.

"Young," I said.

"Word on the street is that Lila likes the older men," Tim said. He winked at me and took a big swig of his bourbon and tapped on the bar—a tune running through his head maybe. I thought about hitting him. Thought about the sound my fist would make against his grizzly chin, about the way his head would snap back, maybe blood would spatter against the fish tank. I took a look at Lila but she was staring forward, far away.

Huan emerged from the back room, cleaning a shot glass with a white towel. "Hey, Huan, I've got a joke for you," Tim said.

"Oh, goodie," Lila snapped back to life, clapping her hands like a little kid. "Is it dirty?"

Tim feigned a frown. "No, it's not dirty. Who do you think I am?"

An asshole, I thought. Huan smiled at all of us, waiting.

"Here goes. A single Chinese guy owns a restaurant, and one day this hot Asian chick walks in."

Lila poked Tim in the side. "Tim, watch yourself."

Tim waved her away. "He immediately walks over and asks her out on a date. She agrees. They go out for a while, and soon, the man proposes to her. She says, 'Yes, but before we do, there's something you must know. I have never had the sex, but I've read about it.' He says no problem, and they get married."

"No problem," echoed Huan, laughing.

Lila groaned, turning to me. "It was nice drinking here while it lasted."

"On their honeymoon, the man tells his wife that since she's a virgin, she can choose what they do first. She says, 'Oh, most honorable husband. I am honored to be your wife, even though I have never had the sex, but I've read about it. So, I have chosen to have the 69.'" Tim was doing a bad accent, really getting into it. "The husband looks confused. He's scratching his head. 'What's wrong?' the wife says, getting nervous. And the guy, he turns and looks at her, all puzzled. 'I don't get it, he says. 'You want…the beef and broccoli?'"

Huan chuckled, pointing his finger at Tim and shaking his head. But Lila, she laughed so hard at the punch line—one I didn't find all that funny, for the record—that I thought for a second she might be choking. Her head rolled back, her arms flailed out in front of her, maybe to slap the edge of the bar, but instead she swiped her tall glass. What was left of the blue liquid sprayed, splashing a bit on Tim's face, and leaving an interesting modern art project on Lila's white skirt.

"Fuck!" Lila screamed, jumping up. "That's cold."

***

Lila asked if I could drive her to my apartment to remove the stain. It was a two hundred dollar skirt, she said. Leather. If she drove the half-hour to her house, it would be ruined.

"Come on," I said. "I wouldn't want it to stain. That skirt costs more than my rent."

Lila followed closely up the stairs. She swayed into me as I fumbled with the keys at the door, and it occurred to me that Lila had maybe had one too many Birds of Paradise. Nevertheless, she righted herself and strolled into the apartment like she owned it, even though it was the first time she'd ever been there.

"Where's Professor?" she asked, circling around with her arms out like she might accidentally step on him. "I've never seen an iguana in person."

"He's probably sleeping," I said, distracted suddenly. Seeing Lila there in the dim light, my apartment seemed very small.

"Well, then I'll take the bathroom first. And something to blot these stains out."

I handed her some corn starch (courtesy of a Google search) and pointed to the bathroom door. While she was in there, I took the opportunity to rinse out the dirty dishes in the sink, straighten up the living room, scanning the place the way you do when an unexpected guest comes in and the piggish way you move through life is suddenly illuminated like The Professor under his heat lamp.

The doorbell rang while Lila was still in the bathroom. I considered not answering it, pretending I didn't hear it, but then I heard Lila from behind the bathroom door say in her high-pitched voice, "Whoooo iz it?"

I opened the door to find Theresa rocking back on her heels, her hair poofed out around her shoulders like a cartoon figure who'd just stuck her finger in an electrical socket. "Hi?" she said, the voice! Everything a question. "I was wondering if I could come in for a few minutes to see The Professor?"

"Oh, not tonight, Theresa. I have a friend over." I checked my watch. It felt a lot later than eight o'clock.

She pouted, rocking again, trying to peer over my shoulder in a way that made me uncomfortable. I closed the door tighter so she couldn't squeeze through.

"I'll just be a minute? Please?"

I shook my head, determined to be firm. About that time, James, the metrosexual from across the hall, whistled his way out of the stairwell. Theresa looked over at him and for a split second I had the urge to shove her toward him, make her his problem. Then she turned back, her voice very loud in the small hall.

"I really want to pet your lizard!" she cried, sounding hysterical in a way I'd never heard. James looked up at me. Our eyes met, and I realized what he was thinking, what he'd just heard. I suppressed a laugh—it caught in my throat and sat there like a baseball. The way James might see it all—the way it could go down—made me feel numb. The Judge, the girl.

"Theresa, another time. *The iguana* is sleeping," I said, emphasis on "the iguana" for James' sake, but the worry had already leaked in. The thought that James might think that something sordid was going on made me act guilty, and suddenly all those times I'd let Theresa into my apartment alone made my skin crawl. What if? *Just this one time.* And Mary Beth, with all her suspicions. I'd never see Megan again.

Of course, all these thoughts went flashing through my brain in a matter of seconds—the time it took for the Judge to weigh his options and make his decision, nonetheless—and so by the time James unlocked his door and went inside to call Child Services and have me locked up I had already given Theresa five other reasons why she couldn't come in. She was staring at me, hurt in her eyes. I hated to disappoint her—she did in some ways remind me of Megan, always searching for approval, waiting to be wounded by everything and anything—and yet she was nothing like my daughter at all, and there was a certain guilt in that as well—in the relief that Megan was normal, socially accepted, all that jazz. Theresa was giving me a headache as she stood there, making that strange sound in her throat, the faint aroma of ammonia wafting off her.

"I'm sorry," I said again, softly, and closed the door in her face. I heard her shuffle back down the hall and congratulated myself on making the right choice, on being firm.

I turned around. Lila had come out of the bathroom. She was standing stark naked in the middle of the living room, hands down at her side. She stared at me, not saying a word, her eyes that same expression I'd seen at the bar.

And that's when I realized it was too late. I'd already let the girl in.

Support

Nati received the first letter from her dead husband just a few days before her daughter and the new baby were coming to stay. It had been eight years since the fishing accident had taken Harold from her, and when she opened the letter it was like reading something dirty, forbidden, and then like she was reading something on fire.

She had heard about these kinds of scams, people preying on widows, making promises, but this? This seemed especially cruel.

She folded the letter and tucked it behind a cookbook in the kitchen. But each time she went into the kitchen to get a glass of water or something to eat, the cookbook stood out like a blinking hazard light. It had been a long time since she'd seen her husband's handwriting, but it did seem familiar to her, a left-leaning chicken scratch scribble with long thin loops that reminded her of orzo. She was worried about her heart, the way this whole thing had worked her up. The cookbook was talking to her, reciting its favorite lines from the letter it his. *It was nothing that you did, Nati. I need you to believe that. I hope you are happy.*

And the timing was just awful now, with Evelyn and the baby coming to visit. The night before they were to arrive, Nati pushed a chair over to the refrigerator and fished out the dusty bottle of Southern Comfort from the cabinet above. She poured some into a milk glass, held her nose, and drank it. After the second glass, she almost had the courage to rip the letter into shreds. But something wouldn't let her.

***

Evelyn arrived on a rainy day. A tropical storm was working its way up the coast, and the steady downpour left pockets of flooded holes in the front yard and forced the cancellation of the church picnic. It was a mess getting the baby and the luggage and all the gear in the house with no men to help, and because of the downpour, Nati didn't even properly greet her daughter until they were inside, soaking wet, the baby in her car seat on the floor between them. "Give me a hug," she said to her daughter, "and let me get my hands on this bundle of precious."

Evelyn seemed in good spirits; much better than she had been when she'd called all those weeks ago in a panic, exhausted and lonely. Her husband had just been deployed to Iraq, missed the birth of Megan Marie, and probably wouldn't be back until at least Thanksgiving. The sides and bottoms of Evelyn's eyes looked dark and thin, but her smile seemed genuine and relieved. She had cut her hair shorter and gotten bangs that made her face look more round and full, even if she kept pushing them off to the side like they annoyed her.

Nati picked up Megan Marie. She had forgotten how tiny they were in the beginning, how quickly their heads could roll back, the delicate, wrinkled, birdlike skin on their necks. The baby didn't even stir; she was fast asleep. "The car ride always does it," Evelyn said. She pushed back on the couch, closed her eyes, and put her feet up on the coffee table, like she'd just stepped from an airplane to a beach resort and was looking for the waiter to bring her a piña colada. "Sometimes I wish I could just hire someone to drive her around for a few hours. Wouldn't that be nice?"

"You probably could, these days," Nati said. "Or maybe right there is your strike-it-rich idea. Baby chauffeurs. Mommy taxis. Think of a cute name and you're all good." She looked down at the baby, bounced her softly. "Hello there, Miss Megan," she said. "How are you today?" She looked over at Evelyn. "And how are you doing? Are you okay?"

"God, I'm starving," Evelyn declared, and hurled herself off the couch and headed for the kitchen. They'd never been close, Nati and her daughter, never in that way that Nati had imagined when she'd thought of having children, of having a daughter—eating chickpea salads at an outdoor café, watching scary movies on the couch, giving fashion advice, sitting on the porch playing gin rummy. Stupid.

Maybe it was her own shortcomings that had done it. Maybe she'd raised Evelyn wrong somehow, or maybe it was the pieces of Harold creeping in. Her husband had never been the warmest man in the world. Nati had loved him more for his strength, his dependability, not for his laughter.

But she was being unfair. Nati and Evelyn had a fine relationship really. After all, with this trouble, in these trying times, Evelyn chose to be with her, to trust her. They may not share hairstyles or cry over sappy movies or carry around pocket mirrors with their initials engraved on the back, but there was a quiet strength to their relationship.

She could hear Evelyn moving around the kitchen in that confident way that she had—taking charge, making herself at home. Nati imagined her putting away groceries she'd bought—probably a special kind of milk, fruit, and snacks bought at some health store—moving Nati's things over to the side or the back of the refrigerator where ice crystals would grow. She didn't mind this so much—there was something comforting about her daughter coming back home—but part of Evelyn's actions also felt brazen, selfish, the way she'd been since she was a girl. That entitlement that kids naturally had: This. Is. Mine.

Nati was relieved that she had hidden The Letter inside that cookbook, wincing as she imagined Evelyn finding it on the counter in all her unpacking and rearranging, ("Well, what is this?" thinking that her mother had once again misplaced some important mail), opening it, reading it (for that was also part of the entitlement—her parents' mail, their private things, there were no boundaries). Nati imagined her daughter's face falling as she read the lines from the letter Nati had by now memorized: *I know you can't understand...I was a different person then...the routine of it all...tired.*

"Your grandpa might still be alive," Nati whispered into the baby's ear. Megan Marie stared up at Nati in that unabashed way that babies have before they learn it isn't polite to do so. "Should we tell your momma?"

"Tell her what?" Evelyn said, affectionately, holding a can of parmesan cheese in her hand that she undoubtedly was going to ask Nati if she could toss out. Expiration date, probably. "What are you two whispering about out here?"

Nati tamped down her irritation and smiled. "Oh nothing, just girl talk," she said, tucking her secret down into her belly.

***

Nati couldn't sleep. She went down to the kitchen, turned on the light above the stove. She pulled closed the flimsy curtains on the window above the sink. Harold could be out there, anywhere—no that was stupid. Whoever wrote that letter could be out there, watching her. Didn't these people go through your garbage? Learn things about you to mess with your head?

Harmony in Seasons was the name of the cookbook, and as she went to find the letter, something else fell loose. A Christmas card stamped with a nativity scene. On the inside that same orzo scribble, and Nati realized with a start that Harold had bought her the book one year for Christmas. She read the note: *This way there will always be harmony, year-round. Love, Harold.*

Harmony. Yeah, right. Nati snorted.

She'd known Harold since high school, but they didn't start dating until a few years later when they were both working at the nearby state fair. She was a ticket-taker at the admissions booth and he helped clean up the midway and the grounds. Later he became one of the best real estate agents around—snagged them a beautiful house on the lake that they otherwise couldn't even have afforded the flood insurance for—and

Nati opened a lingerie store in town, specializing in bridal items and special fit bras for women with mastectomies or other breast issues. Hers was the only specialty shop of its kind for miles around, and she really hit it big time when a young television star in a popular sitcom heard about her shop and came in on her vacation to buy undergarments for her wedding day. All the local TV stations had come out to do interviews. Nati and Harold had watched the segment later that night, and she'd been embarrassed by how flushed her face looked, how shaky her hands seemed.

Harold developed a love of fishing. He bought a boat and then a custom fishing pole. He always wanted to take Evelyn out with him, but she grew bored after a few minutes and wanted to suntan. Nati herself was never much of a water bug, and she hated the sun—got rashes from it—so Harold took to booking bigger excursions with other men. Deep-sea fishing, cruises, whale watching. It was on one of those deep-sea expeditions that he'd fallen overboard in the night. By the time the crew realized he was missing, it was too late. They never recovered his body.

Nati had always been mildly unsettled by that, but she'd never thought anything suspicious about it. Now, everything sounded like a Lifetime movie that that young actress might've starred in.

With dread she pulled out the more recent note, tucked between the pages of a Symphony Veggie Pasta recipe. She put the two together. The handwriting was exactly the same, and Nati felt her heartbeat increase in her chest. She was suddenly in the middle of a very bad dream.

She re-read the note again, this time slower. There wasn't much there—not those details she wanted. Not the reasons. *I am alive,* he wrote—on one separate line, as if for drama. And then later, *I'm sorry for the shock this will cause you. I'm not even sure why I'm writing to you now except that I think you should know, I think Evelyn should know.* And then even later, *I am sorry.*

Nati went through a series of emotions while reading it. Anger, then excitement, a weird flutter of the heart. Then utter depression—the mention of Evelyn's name—how dare he even use it, how dare he even think he could bring her into it, hurt her all over again. The sheer over-whelming memory of the funeral. She could still remember the pinch of those heels she wore that day, that constant ache in her toes, and the way the backs of those blasted cheap things had rubbed her ankles raw. The two dried pools of blood on the back of her pantyhose.

Evelyn, home from her sophomore year of college, took to drinking directly from a bottle of Southern Comfort (Harold had liked to put it in his tea) out on the back porch, earphones on, but the music so loud Nati could hear it in the kitchen—a fast, driving beat. How she'd debated about taking the alcohol away! How she'd considered going out there, pulling off the earphones and giving her daughter a hug. Or taking a seat across from her and stealing a swig from the bottle herself. She'd considered all those things, standing in her bare, scarred feet in the kitchen that day, watching her daughter's head sway slowly back and forth on the porch swing. And she'd done none of them. She'd left Evelyn alone out there, convincing herself that was the best way for them to deal with their grief. Each in her own way.

Nati went over to the sink. Through the window she could see that same porch swing Evelyn had sat on that night. And beyond that, the shed where Nati had found her months later, after Evelyn had dropped out of school for a semester to pull herself together, setting fire to pic-tures. The solution that time was therapy. And it had worked. Evelyn had gone back to school, graduated, worked for a while as a counselor for battered women down in Salem. But the absence of Harold had never brought them any closer. If anything, he left an even bigger hole between them, and they both seemed unable to fill it.

***

Just an hour or so before closing the next night, a woman walked into Nati's shop. "Can I help you?" Nati asked, perhaps a little too aggressively, as she'd been hoping to close up early to go home to Evelyn and the baby.

"I guess...I need a fitting," the woman said, stepping back, her head turning back and forth. She was a jumpy one, with a thin face, dark olive skin, and green cat eyes. "I need a bra...I need something. I recently had a mastectomy."

Ah, so that was it. Nati nodded, immediately taking charge. "Of course. Come over here," she said, leading the way. This was her favorite kind of customer, someone who really needed her. She'd never wanted to just sell things—she always envisioned it as more, as truly helping women. It was why she named the store Support: A Boutique for Women, with a pretty pink bra outlining the rounded part of the two "P"s in the sign. Over the years, Nati had become good friends with some of her customers—a bridge group here, dinner parties there. She found the whole thing, well, rewarding was the word she used when she talked about it. But really, it made her feel less lonely. A part of something bigger.

"Is this your first fitting?"

The woman blushed, nodded. "I've...I should've come a while ago, I guess, but I..." she stopped, turned around, and gazed at the racks of bras like a tourist lost in a giant museum of art.

"Absolutely. It takes a bit of time," Nati said. "Now, did you have a full or partial?"

The woman exhaled. "Partial. The right breast."

Nati leaned over, squeezed the woman's hand. "We're going to take care of you. Don't you worry. Goodness, you are so beautiful! Let's find something that will make you feel that way." Her name was Veronica, a name as delicate as the woman herself.

***

When Nati got home, she was careful to open the front door quietly. Earlier in the week she'd come in and woken the baby, who had just settled down in her bassinet.

The living room was empty, but Nati could hear Megan Marie crying in the kitchen at the back of the house. Nati slid off her coat and headed that way. Evelyn was standing, rocking the baby, her back to Nati, head tilted to cup the house phone with her shoulder. "No, no," Nati heard her say sharply. "It's fine. I'll just talk to you later." She turned, hung up the phone, and let out a sharp scream. "My god, mother! You scared the hell out of me."

"I'm sorry," Nati blushed.

"What are you doing sneaking around like that?"

"I'm not," Nati said, annoyed now. Evelyn seemed tense, jumpy, like Nati had caught her doing something bad. "Who was on the phone?"

"No one," Evelyn said. She gestured toward Megan. "Do you mind trying? She's been doing this forever."

Nati scooped up the baby and began bouncing her. Nati was concerned by her daughter's reaction to her question about the phone call. She felt a crack of fear. What if that had been Harold? After all, Evelyn had a cell phone. Why would she be using the house phone unless...unless someone had called the number. And no one ever called Nati.

Evelyn left the kitchen, so Nati followed her out to the living room. "Was it someone for me?" Nati asked again. Evelyn was sitting on the couch, tugging on the ends of her hair. She looked up blankly. "What?"

"The phone. Was it someone for me?" Nati felt the panic flushing up her neck. So he'd called, spoken to Evelyn. Did Evelyn know that Nati knew? Was she trying to hide it from her?

"No," Evelyn said, shaking her head. "It wasn't for you." She looked like she was going to say more, but stopped. Evelyn seemed far away, lost in thought, as if Nati wasn't even there. Nati fought the urge to ask again.

Megan's cries had subsided for a brief moment, but started up again when she saw her mother. Maybe, Nati thought, Evelyn was just exhausted from taking care of an infant. "I think she's hungry," Nati said, almost apologetically.

"She's always hungry." Evelyn's eyes looked wet, like she was trying to hold back tears. "Give her here." Nati saw Evelyn wince in pain as the baby latched on to her breast.

"You need to come into the store. We have some really lovely nursing bras," Nati said, trying not to watch, trying to curb her urge to go over to help. Nati sat down in the rocking chair on the other side of the room, unsure what to do. She had tried to broach the subject of bottle feeding—just trying it—but Evelyn had seemed very upset by the idea, so Nati shut up about it. She knew the drill: the worst mistake as a grandparent is to dispense unwanted advice.

Finally the baby latched on and Evelyn's body relaxed some, leaned back on the couch. "You need to tell me something interesting," Evelyn said. "Distract me or something."

Nati was at a loss. She was amazed that Evelyn had decided to have children. Her daughter had, even from childhood, always managed to draw an imaginary circle around herself, never allowing anyone in. Evelyn never had a best friend growing up—she always just drifted in and out of groups, invited to parties and gatherings, but never attending them with any drive or passion. The relationships she got in only seemed to get close when one or the other was going away to college—and then the string of Internet boyfriends, all from states or countries very far away. Then there was the married man, the one that Nati didn't like to talk about, the one that she still prayed on the rosary that Evelyn would never cross paths with again. And finally Evelyn met Mark, her husband, a military man called to duty every few years.

When Nati pointed out the pattern, so obvious to her, Evelyn's response was to shut down—a reaction clearly perfect for a person who doesn't want to hear about their problems with intimacy.

"This is not a very good story," Evelyn joked, wiping her bangs out of her face with her free hand, and Nati realized she'd just been quietly staring into space.

"I'm sorry, I'm sorry," she said. "I was thinking—I was just thinking about your father," Nati said, then immediately regretted bringing him up.

"What about him?" Evelyn said.

"He used to sit up with you in the middle of the night, listening to radio programs. You loved listening to the radio."

Evelyn smiled. "That's nice."

"What would you say to him if he walked in here right now?" Nati asked.

"I don't know if I'd say anything. I think I would just show him M&M here and that would be all he needed," Evelyn said. "A granddaughter. He'd be so over the moon." She laughed, looked up at the ceiling like she was imagining the whole scene. Nati tensed. She was about to get up, go to the kitchen, and bring the letter in to Evelyn. "Why? What would you do, Ma?"

"I'd ask him where the hell he's been these past eight years."

Evelyn laughed. "Oh mom, you're so literal."

***

Nati's full-time assistant, Patricia, was blathering on while they stacked piles of new merchandise—black silk bras with front closures. Nati kept rubbing her fingers across the soft fabric as she worked.

"So how is your visit with your daughter going?" Patricia asked.

"Oh, you know. It's good. It's fine. It's so lovely having the baby around."

"Oh, I bet it is," Patricia smiled. But no, she probably didn't know. Patricia did not like children. She and her husband didn't have any kids, made a show of talking about that decision very publicly—how much they liked to travel, go to shows, eat out. As if having a child sentenced you to a lifetime of television sitcoms and yardwork. "Just enjoy it while you can. They grow up so fast, you know."

Enjoy it while you can. Harold used to say things like that, those platitudes that meant a whole lot of nothing. He was good at smooth talking, which was why he always was able to close that sale, make those families feel like they were buying more than just a house. They were buying a future together. A life. He loved to watch this one segment on the local news—a newscaster who just picked a name at random from the local phonebook, called the person, and did a story on his or her life. Harold used to always shake his head, nearly tear up, and say, "Everyone's got a story, Nati. Everyone."

"It's amazing how you can never really know another person, isn't it?" Nati asked Patricia, tucking the bras into drawers underneath the display. She liked having things arranged neatly. It felt like an accomplishment.

"Oh yeah, I know exactly what you mean. Peter—we've been married for how long? Eighteen years? And all this time the man hates peanut butter. Loathes peanut butter. 'Don't come near me with that,' he says. Won't even want it in the house. I come down for breakfast the other morning and what's he doing? Slathering Jiffy all over his toast. Like it's going out of style. I mean, really?"

"But I mean the inside of people. Like, true thoughts, motivations. You hear those stories all the time about the serial killers and how their wives never even knew. You just never know." She kept thinking about all those fishing trips Harold took, one every month, like clockwork. How she never even thought to check up on him, if he really was where he said he was going.

"Well, I highly doubt anyone I know is a serial killer," Patricia said with a snort. Patricia would be the woman that the television newscaster would pick from random out of the phone book, Nati thought. He would never choose Nati, but Patricia, she was the type of woman that just had that kind of luck.

That was the problem with those kinds of things, Nati thought—you can twist anything around to make it seem good.

***

The second letter came on the back of a postcard:

Lulu,
You are probably feeling very overwhelmed right now with my contact. I
am sorry. I know this is hard, and I don't even know what I will say to you
when I see you.
Harold

The postcard was a picture of Bash Bish Falls, one of the places they'd visited on their honeymoon in Massachusetts all those years ago. One end of the postcard was frayed from handling at the post office, but it was definitely a new postcard, bought recently. She imagined Harold standing at the falls, remembering their honeymoon, the creaky bed in the only hotel room they could afford at the time, those cherry pastries they shared at a picnic in the park. She imagined him now—older? wrinkly?—rooting through the postcards in the park's gift shop. Was he revisiting all their favorite landmarks?

And "Lulu"? Had he ever called her that? It sounded familiar somehow and yet it didn't. Harold had never been one for nicknames, really. Not in their later years together anyway.

She began to get hung up on trivial things. Like how much more it would cost her at the grocery store if she had to buy food for both of them again. And how he'd never really liked mushrooms—she'd been eating portabellas regularly now for eight years—how would that work? A very jagged resentment poked at her insides. *No way, Jose.* If he had done this to her, he was going to have to deal with the way things have changed since he'd been gone. She went to book club night. She didn't drink much. And yes, she slept with three different pillows and the down comforter on top of her no matter how hot it was outside.

Nati kept trying to tell Evelyn, but it came out all wrong and she chickened out. "Evelyn, about your father. I think he's here," she said one night while they were watching *Wheel of Fortune.*

"No, you dummy. Don't buy a vowel." Evelyn turned to her mother. "Oh ma, really?"

Nati was puzzled by the sympathy in Evelyn's voice, but she continued. "I just—I don't know for sure, but I think he's...around. He might be coming here."

"Mom, this happened to a friend of mine's mother after her husband died. I think it's totally normal. You see things—you want to see things. Sometimes it happens right after the death, but sometimes it happens years later."

Ghosts. So Evelyn thought she was seeing ghosts. Nati laughed at the thought of Harold haunting her. Closing doors. Leaving dishes in the sink. She shook her head. "Never mind. It's stupid."

"It's not stupid, Ma," Evelyn said sleepily, lying back against the couch. "You just miss him is all."

***

The third letter came a week later in a plain white envelope. It didn't address her at all. It simply said: *I'm coming to see you on Wednesday. I hope you will let me explain things. If you don't answer, I'll know what to do. H*

Wednesday.

She carried around this knowledge like a giant wart on her face. Every reference someone made to time, Nati felt self-conscious, nervous, ashamed. Patricia said, "Those shipments of strapless bras are coming on Friday—do I need to come in over the weekend to help with them?" and all Nati could think was that by then, she would know if this was all true or not. She and Evelyn were watching a game show on television and one of the commercials advertised a new show starting Wednesday evening— maybe Harold would be there watching it with them.

But she didn't miss him. Evelyn was wrong. She was anxious, angry, sure, curious, but miss him? She wanted to smack him clear across the face and tell him where he could shove his notes.

***

When Veronica came in to pick up her special order, she asked to try on the bras before buying them and blushed deep as though she was asking something inappropriate. Nati set her up in the biggest of the dressing rooms and left her there. She got caught up with several other customers and phone calls, and a good while passed before Nati remembered Veronica again. She went back to check on her. The door to the changing room was still closed. Nati tapped with her knuckles. "Everything going okay in there?"

"Yes, thank you." Veronica's voice was falsely cheerful, but she sounded like she had acquired a sudden cold.

"Are you sure?"

"No."

Nati opened the door and saw Veronica crying on the bench in the bra (which fit wonderfully, Nati noticed).

"What's wrong, dear?"

She shook her head.

"It looks gorgeous on you," Nati said, but that made her cry even harder. Nati sat down beside her, patted her hand.

"It's been half a year now. And this is the first time I'm coming—this is the first time I've actually cared at all…" she looked up at Nati. "He's never seen—he doesn't know."

"A new man?"

Veronica nodded, blushed. She had an interesting way of blushing—dark and scarlet. It spread quickly like a rash up the woman's neck and into her cheeks.

"If he's worth his salt, it won't matter a lick."

"Oh god, it has to matter, doesn't it?" Veronica looked down at herself. "I mean, what if it does matter?"

Nati shook her head. "I don't know. I guess he's not worth it then."

"And what if he's mad I kept the secret for so long? Oh my." She started crying again, worse this time, a wave of red nose and watery eyes. "Oh my, look at me. Oh, I'm so sorry. I just. Well, it's just."

"People can surprise you all the time," Nati said. "Do you want to hear a crazy story?"

Veronica nodded.

"My husband, he was—he is—a fisherman, always liked that sort of thing. He disappeared eight years ago and everyone thought he was dead." She paused. "But he's not."

Veronica looked puzzled through her tears. "How do you know?"

"He contacted me. He had to pretend he was dead all this time because he had bad people after him. Gambling debts." Harold always did like his monthly poker games; it could be true.

Veronica's eyes were wide. "So you didn't know?"

Nati shook her head.

"What are you going to do?"

Nati shrugged.

"Aren't you mad? I would be…but, I mean, if you're not mad, then maybe he won't be mad at me. It's been like two months. He's starting to suspect something's wrong, I know. I should've told him." She sighed. "Oh, you don't think he'll be mad, do you?"

"I have no idea what he'll be," Nati said, thinking about Harold. And what if he didn't want to come back home? All this time, in a snuff about him wanting back in, the gall of it all—but what if he didn't want back in? Nati felt fear flickering in her belly. What would she do then? "But if he doesn't want you, then he's damn fool stupid."

Veronica frowned, back in her own thoughts and problems. Nati regretted saying anything at all to her. "I thought I was dead," Veronica mumbled. She fingered the lace of one of the gowns and sighed. "Anyway, thanks for your help and all. I'm just—I'll finish up here. I'm sorry to take up your time."

"You're not—it's fine. Just take your time," Nati said. She felt irritated with Veronica and with herself. *But didn't you just hear what I told you? My husband is* alive. That newscaster man would've cared. He would've told her story, and maybe she would contact him herself one of these days. Maybe this Veronica would see the story on TV and then she would realize.

***

When Nati came home from the store Wednesday, Evelyn was already making dinner. "I thought I'd surprise you," she said, seeming more cheerful than the previous days. She licked sauce off the spoon and set it down next to the baby monitor on the counter. "It's this spaghetti squash recipe I've been meaning to try. Spaghetti squash and meatballs."

"Oh, sounds good," Nati said. Her stomach was so in knots she wasn't sure she could eat one crumb of bread, but she didn't want to disappoint her daughter. Evelyn was whistling as she puttered around the kitchen. Whistling! Imagine if she knew what could happen tonight! Evelyn turned and smiled, and Nati felt even worse about not telling her before, not preparing her. There had just never been a good time.

"Go ahead. Get changed or whatever. It should be ready when you come back down."

She went upstairs. She tried throwing up, but there was nothing. She hadn't eaten all day.

In the closet, she sifted through her clothes, irritated. Everything seemed dowdy, ugly, plain. Or on the other stratosphere, too fancy. Wouldn't Evelyn be surprised if Nati came downstairs wearing a sequined gown she'd bought for a wedding three years ago? She settled for a nicer blouse with a cityscape of Paris and her nicest pair of jeans.

No need to dress up, anyway, she reminded herself. Not for him. Why did he deserve that?

Still, she felt silly refreshing her makeup, like this was some date. She looked at herself in the mirror. Old. What had she looked like eight years ago? Would he be disappointed? Would she? "Ridiculous," she said again to her reflection. "You are the dumbest broad on the block."

On her way downstairs, Nati heard a loud ding from Evelyn's room. She had left her computer on. Ding. Ding. Again the noise. Nati went in, the blue light of the screen making everything seem a little distorted. There was a small box open in the middle of the screen. Tiny conversation bubbles were popping up one after the other, each one sending a loud 'ding' into the room. Before she could decide what to do, if anything, she couldn't help but notice the words on the screen, labeled from "Ben," Evelyn's husband's name.

I'm sorry.

I know it's hard 4 u, especially so far away.

I still want 2 B in MMs life.

Nati backed away, her face flushed like she'd been caught doing something bad.

Downstairs, Evelyn had the table set with the nice china. Her daughter's cheerfulness now seemed false to Nati, the smiles forced. Were her eyes a bit puffy? "We should eat before she wakes up," Evelyn said. She held up a bottle of red wine. "Drinks!"

"What is all this fuss for?"

Evelyn shrugged. "I felt like cooking. Is that okay?"

"Of course." Nati forced herself to smile. "This will be great."

"Yes!"

They ate quickly, Evelyn constantly looking at the monitor for any sign of movement.

"Are you okay?" Nati asked her. She thought about what she'd seen on the computer. She didn't know much about technology, sure, but some things didn't need fancy computer programs to come through.

Something had happened. Something bad. And Evelyn didn't want to talk about it.

"Of course," Evelyn said, too fast. She had a glass of wine, took a large drink from it. "Why?"

"Just want to make sure."

"Are *you* okay?"

"Yes."

They sat there. Nati filled the wine glasses again. It seemed painful, the silence. All this between them, seeping into the air. It made Nati think of the time, after Harold's 40th birthday party, that he'd accidentally knocked an entire bottle of red wine off the dining room table. She'd dabbed and dabbed at the stain, but it had never really come out. *Just tell her*, she thought. *Tell her.*

"I'm glad you came," Nati said finally. "It's nice to have you both here."

Evelyn nodded in that distracted way Nati was becoming used to. "I'm so tired."

"Babies will do that to you."

Evelyn sighed, ran her fingers through her bangs. "Tired. Overwhelmed." She sat back in her chair, looked up at the ceiling. "Did you ever want to…ever wish you could go back and do everything different?"

"What?" Nati laughed anxiously. "No. Not really."

"Well, not everything." Evelyn looked into Nati's eyes, very serious, focused. "Just…some stuff. Just—wish you could go back and do things over, see what else might've happened."

My god, Nati thought. Why didn't I tell her before? What is wrong with me? Always with the "leave it alone, it will all work itself out" mentality. She felt like someone had set fire to the middle of her back. Panic.

Evelyn was still talking. "I'm just…I feel like a terrible mother. All the time. I feel like—a terrible person. I just wish…"

"Oh, Evelyn, everyone feels that way sometimes." She leaned forward, put her hand awkwardly on top of her daughter's. She was surprised at her own gesture, surprised too when Evelyn flipped her own hand and squeezed Nati back. She could hardly believe her daughter was talking to her about this, and now, of all times. She didn't know what to say, but Evelyn didn't seem to mind.

"Everybody? Really?" Her eyes flooded suddenly with tears. "Did you ever…It's just, sometimes I feel so angry. So tired."

"This is all normal, it's all just an adjustment. You'll be fine." She leaned over then and hugged Evelyn. Over Evelyn's shoulder, she saw the portrait of the three of them that the church had taken many years ago. Evelyn smiling with a mouthful of braces, Harold with that big goofy grin he used to always give for pictures. "It's the good people, the strong people, that stick through the hard times," Nati said to the portrait.

Evelyn was crying harder now. Nati got up to get a box of tissues. "Oh, mom—I don't know what I'm going to do," Evelyn said, blowing her nose.

The doorbell rang. Nati met Evelyn's eyes. Her heart was pounding in her chest. She felt it all unraveling there before her, all of it, like a big ball of yarn down a hill that she couldn't catch. She leaned across and squeezed Evelyn's hand. "It's going to be all right. I promise." Trying to convince both of them, maybe.

She thought about what Evelyn had said about going back, doing it all over. See what else might've happened. She thought of an article she'd read once—some science fiction piece or philosophy—something about all the different worlds out there that disappear every time you make a decision, all the doors that close that you can never go back to.

The doorbell rang a second time. Evelyn pulled her hand away, wiped her eyes with her sleeve. "Mom, you should get that."

Nati looked up at the picture again. She saw the doors, the universes, flash before her eyes—all of them, all at once. All the stories that newscaster would never write, dissolving like a Kleenex in water. And all the other possibilities opening up, unfolding like a flower. For all the times before when she didn't know what to do, this time everything was perfectly clear.

Nati shook her head at Evelyn. "Nope," she said. "Whoever it is, it's not important. You were telling me something." She tipped the wine bottle and topped off both their glasses. "So go ahead. It's just you and me. I'm listening."

Scabs

These days Jack only stopped by the house to visit Ma when he knew his father was out drinking. He handed her his copy of *The Times Leader* and she sat down, adjusting her reading glasses. She always went through the pages looking for his byline. "Word is they're bringing in more security," she said.

"Probably," he said. "Ever since they took the fence down, the picketers have been trying to come around the back entrance again."

Ma always had food ready for him. This time it was haluski, and the smell of butter and cabbage made Jack's stomach growl. He'd missed that when he was away at college, one of the only things he'd missed about home.

Ma pulled her glasses to the tip of her nose and looked up at him. "Are you okay, Jack?"

He took from the cabinet an old McDonald's glass with Mickey Mouse's face faded into the side, and opened the freezer for ice. "Dad still eats all those TV dinners all the time?"

"I only buy them when they're on sale."

"They must be on sale all the time then," Jack said.

"Have they been bothering you at your new apartment?" she persisted, and something in her voice made him turn.

"Have they been bothering *you* again?"

"That's not what I—"

"Ma? Have they been calling again?"

She shook her head. "Well, just once. The other night. Your father answered it."

"What did they say?"

"I don't know. He wouldn't tell me."

Jack turned back, trying not to get angry. He imagined his father answering the phone. *Your son's a goddamn scab.* It was better his father answered it than Ma, though it probably affected his dad more. Jack working for the newspaper despite the union strike fueled the fire and bruised his father's ego at the same time.

Jack studied the refrigerator, always covered in magnets and clippings and photos. A photo of him from childhood carrying his favorite toy frog that he slept with until its stuffing came out. More recent photos of cousins. A story about five ways to reduce stress. A cross that someone had made out of yarn and a plastic grid. Prayer cards, and a schedule for St. Mary's special masses. A handwritten note by his dad that read, "Don't use to much electricity." The spelling error annoyed him, and he thought about correcting it just to piss his dad off.

"So he's still being stubborn about everything?"

Ma shrugged, looked down. The newspaper rustled between her hands. "I don't know if stubborn's the word, Jackie."

"Bull, Ma. Bull."

"Jackie, not in this house. Please. We've heard enough these last few weeks."

The anger in his mother's voice worried him. He couldn't have her abandon him as well. Not now. Not after everything. "Ma," he said softly. "You've got to tell me if they keep bothering you, okay? I thought moving out would stop it. I'm sorry."

She smiled. "I'm fine, Jackie. You know that. We're all fine."

But they weren't, not really. Jack wished he hadn't needed to come back to Wilkes-Barre after college. It was the last thing he'd wanted to do—admit defeat. Let his dad see him vulnerable.

His father liked to frequent the American Legion, where he and all the other veterans would sit on fake leather stools, drink foamy beer in the middle of the afternoon, and complain about injustices that didn't really affect them. Lately, Jack imagined, many of those conversations revolved around the newspaper strike. Jack pictured his dad rattling on to the boys about his no-good son and betrayal.

What it is, is: The bottom line is that it's all about the bottom line.

"Come sit here. Eat," Ma said, and Jack complied. The cabbage and noodles were steaming. He added loads of salt and pepper, stuffed large forkfuls down his mouth. "You need more meat on your bones," she said.

Ma could use some muscle herself, he thought. She was so fragile, barely five feet tall. He and his dad used to joke they could use her to bench press if they wanted to take it easy on the workout.

"You're coming to your great-grandmother's party?"

Damn. He'd completely forgotten about it. His great-grandmother Ursula was turning ninety-five. No one thought she was going to make it to 100, so they wanted to celebrate while they could. It had been planned for months, since before the strike. Jack hadn't even been out in public in Wilkes-Barre for weeks. It had been too dangerous.

"Please tell me you're coming, Jackie."

"Ma, I don't think they want me there."

What it is, is: We'd all be dead, non-existent, if it weren't for the unions.

"Of course he wants you there. Don't be like that. It's just—it's just, well you know how he is."

"Yeah, Ma, I know."

What it is, is you know nothin' about it.

As if conjuring him up with his thoughts, Jack heard the familiar growl of his father's '69 Chevy coming down the street. Ma looked at him, her eyes worried.

"I should go," he said, reluctantly getting up from his half-eaten food.

She shook her head. "No, Jackie, stay. He'll want to see you."

Jack snorted. "You know that's not true." He grabbed the copy of *The Times Leader* and tucked it under his arm. Then he kissed Ma on the cheek. "I'll slip out the back. Thanks for the food."

***

The employees of *The Times Leader* had walked out on October 6, 1978—just about three weeks before Jack started working there as a general news reporter—but the tensions had been brewing since before Jack had moved back to the area. It was why he'd come on board—they needed reporters to keep the place running, and they were willing to pay well. In the very beginning—when they were shuttling reporters back and forth from the Woodlands hotel to the newsroom because it was too dangerous for them to drive—Jack thought it would all blow over pretty quickly. He wasn't prepared for the rage, and he didn't understand it. He'd seen grown men hurling themselves on the tops of moving cars and screaming obscenities at young women. He'd had his tires slashed twice. But after all that, he was still astonished as it continued, escalated.

His father understood those men, though. He'd been a union guy his whole life, and Jack's grandfather a coal miner. They were as loyal to the unions as they were to god and country.

What it is, is: If not for the unions, your PaPa would be dead.

He had heard the stories about his grandfather. Long hours in the mines, dangerous conditions, coming home head-to-toe black as night, blending into the shadows of the house. How he would scrub off all the soot in the bathtub, leaving trails of black tar like tire tracks in the morning. How the unions had saved him, had saved Jack's dad, too, when he got his first job in the mines, saved them from dropping dead of carbon monoxide poisoning, saved them from getting axed for no reason.

"What it is, is protection," said Jack's father. "Loyalty. Didn't they teach you any of that in your fancy college?"

Jack had often imagined his father sitting in one of the lecture halls on campus, listening to a philosophy professor expound upon Marx's theory of human nature. He imagined him squinting at a Richard Hamilton collage at the pop art exhibit in the art gallery, leaning forward, chewing on the edge of his unlit Kool cigarette, mumbling, "What the Christ is he doing anyway?"

As absurd as it was to imagine his father in college, Jack suspected his father thought he was just as out of place back here in Wilkes-Barre. That he equated Jack with the "fancy foreigners" as he called them, editors and writers brought in from New York and Chicago, mostly, who came in and took over the paper and thought they could *run it their own way, with no regard for the people here, for the way things are done.*

"The way it is, is, no one around here wants their bull—we want the way it's been—a family business. No one cares about family anymore, though. It's every man for himself out there." He spoke this passionately, the wheeze from his lungs getting in the way, making him stop every once in a while for a fit of coughing. "They want to break up the Brotherhood. Make us weak, split apart." He talked about it like he had something at stake, when really he was just a long-time subscriber, an old man in his boxers and socks sitting on the back porch in the morning, smoking cigarettes and checking the Phillies stats and the police blotter and the obits for anyone he knew. But for him, it was a war. And Jack was the enemy.

***

When Jack got to the newsroom Friday morning, there was a lot of commotion. The reporters were all gathered around the Metro desk, and Jack had to nudge his way through to see what was going on.

"They're going to be so mad."

"Who cares?"

"My god, it seems quieter already."

"I kind of miss the honking."

They were all admiring a sign that spanned across three desks. Frank Shemanski, the metro editor, sat on the edge of the desk, hands crossed, smirking. He saw Jack and clapped. "Jackie! Take a look! Take a look! I told you I would get it and I never ever go back on my word."

"Can you believe it?" Sophie Kerchak, one of the reporters, asked him. "These boneheads managed to swipe it right from under their noses."

The sign read: HONK IF YOU SUPPORT US in shaky handwriting and big block letters. It had been created by the picketers and propped at the edge of the burning barrel outside *The Times Leader* office for the last few weeks. After days of nearly constant HONK HONK HONK echoing through the newsroom, Shemanski and a few others had sworn that come hell or high water they were going to steal that damn sign.

"Fab, Shemanski. You're a genius," Jack said. "How in the world?"

"Ah-ha, a magician never reveals his secrets."

Jack high-fived him. "All right, man. We need to hang this up."

"Yes!"

"Right in the middle of the newsroom!"

"They're just going to make another one, damn it."

"But we have the original!"

"Now you have to get the burning barrel."

In the middle of the commotion, Mike Jones, the managing editor, stood next to Jack and slapped his back. "You got your first death threat, Jack. Welcome to the club." Jones handed an open package to Jack. It was addressed to him, but had looked suspicious enough that the guys in the mailroom had already opened it.

It was a copy of a headshot of Jack taken in high school at a Rotary Club event (how had someone even found that?) with a knife pasted above his heart and a little cartoon bubble that said, "I'm a SCAB!"

"Hoyt Library," Jones said, and Jack looked up at him.

"What?"

"Library, most likely. The copy looks like it was taken off a micro-film machine. Someone did their homework on you." He chuckled. "I'm required to ask if you would like a detail."

"What?" It was all he could seem to muster. Jack was still trying to process. The image of his smiling face with a knife pointing at it was disarming.

"A cop. Following you around. For your protection." Someone behind him pulled the paper out of his hand, started showing it around the news-room. There was a bulletin board where they tacked up the best ones. And he'd heard the photographers had a pool betting on who would be next. It had become a rite of passage, a joke. So far, no one had actually been hurt—not yet.

"Oh, uh." He was having a hard time listening. Next to him, Crighton, the night editor, was typing on one of the terminals, asking Sophie a question about a story he was reading, oblivious to the com-motion. Always a stickler for the work. "So is it effect or affect?" he asked her, his face squinting so close to the screen that Jack wor-ried the guy's glasses were going to clack against it. Behind him, two reporters looked down through the window at the picketers. "Don't be a hero," one of them said, and then they both groaned loudly, reacting to whatever was outside. In the corner off by himself, Harold Gufstaski, a sports reporter who always wore some type of Phillies apparel, ate yogurt out of a Mason jar while he listened to a game on his transistor radio.

"We've got extra cops around the building already, but we could get someone to follow you home, that sort of thing. Jaserski's got one, for obvious reasons—" a brick had been thrown through Jaserski's front window at home—"so just let me know. Company policy now."

"I think I'll be all right," Jack said.

"Well, at least let some guys walk you out tonight."

When Jones left, Sophie handed him back the paper. "I thought you'd want this for your scrapbook," she said.

"Yeah, thanks." He wasn't in the mood to laugh. He sat down at his desk and rubbed his forehead.

She sat down next to him, her knee brushing against his jacket. She smiled, trying to comfort him, he imagined.

Sophie's boyfriend, who had been a photographer at the paper, had walked out on the first day, and as far as Jack knew, he and Sophie hadn't spoken since. But the opportunities—especially for the women on staff—were too great to pass up for those who'd crossed. It had become an Us against Them mentality. The newsroom was its own bunker in Vietnam, and there was no way the enemy was going to win. Any one of them would probably kill for the others right now.

"A couple of us are going over to the Treadway in Scranton tonight for drinks. You should come, Jack."

He nodded. "I would, but I've got this family thing."

"Oh, that sounds like a blast." She sat back in the chair and fiddled with a ring on her middle finger. "Skip it."

"I can't. It's my great-grandmother's ninety-fifth birthday. I think it's illegal in at least forty-nine states to miss something like that."

She nodded. "Yes, but surely your grammie doesn't stay up late. So you should come over after and see us. We miss you after all. You never hang out with us anymore."

"Way to guilt-trip a man that's just been given a death threat." But she was right. Jack hadn't been much of a joiner lately. He'd used the excuse of moving, but it was everything that was getting him down.

"But you'll try, right? For me?"

"Sure, I'll try," he said, but they both knew he wasn't serious.

***

The family had rented out the American Legion for Grandma Ursula's birthday celebration. Even though the employees had tried to clean it up, you couldn't help but notice the stench of stale cigars and cheap beer permeating the place. Jack came alone, late, and most everyone else was already there, getting drunk and stuffing themselves on the pigs in a blanket and chicken fingers set up on the buffet table against the far wall. He grabbed a punch glass and filled it to the top, scanning the crowd.

He ran into his mother and Aunt Anita first. They were standing with an older man Jack didn't recognize. His aunt's dyed red hair stood in ringlets around her head, and as she smiled, pink lipstick smudged the tips of her teeth. "Jackie, honey, I want you to meet Mr. Highton. He's been my neighbor now for twenty-five years." She looked up at Highton, who was sipping something the color of maraschino cherry juice. "Jack here is Stanley's boy. He went to Columbus."

She meant Columbia, but she was already a little tipsy and he didn't bother to correct her. He saw his mom's lips turn up in a smile, but she didn't make eye contact with him. Jack smiled up at Highton, who was very tall, and saluted him. Highton looked like he didn't know a university from a historical figure anyway. He smelled like Old Spice and looked slightly dim, like he was floating on the effects of some good drugs. "To the Niña, the Pinta, and the Santa Maria," Jack said.

"Thank you for coming," his ma whispered in his ear. "You're a good boy."

"I don't know about that," Jack said.

"Your father's downstairs with the boys and the beer," his mother told him. "You should go say hello."

It was the last thing he wanted to do, but before he could say anything, Highton coughed loudly and touched his aunt on the shoulder. "You know, Anita, that Milton's boy just finished law school? I remember when that kid was running through our legs chasing dog tails." He laughed, shook his head. "Time flies." He blinked, and nodded at Jack. "So what are you doing now, Jack?"

So he didn't know. His ma blushed. Highton would have an opinion about the strike—and from his mother's expression it wouldn't be a favorable one. She turned and pointed to the dance floor. "Look, Benson! Is that Marie on the dance floor? Look at her go."

He silently blessed his ma and because she'd saved him, he did as she asked and excused himself to get a beer. The keg was in the base-ment—a back room, concrete floor, away from Grandma Ursula's eyes. She didn't like the alcohol, so it was just better if she didn't see it.

Jack's father was leaning against the back wall with a full plastic cup, and Jack's uncles formed a semi-circle around the keg. They had been talking loudly, voices echoing off the bare walls, but when they saw him, they stopped. They focused on him, and the cold of the basement seeped through Jack's clothes. The bare lightbulb hanging from the ceiling made the whole place feel like an interrogation room. Despite the cold, Jack began to sweat.

"Need a refill?" Uncle Maury asked, his Northeast PA accent thick. Jack hadn't ever noticed how they all talked—syllables all squished together, cut-off ends of words—until he'd left for awhile and come back. He didn't like the way Uncle Maury was smiling at him, but Jack handed over his empty punch glass anyway.

Uncle Maury took it, tilted it, shook his head. "Real fancy glass, eh? None of this plastic cup stuff for Jackie, huh boys?"

From the back, his dad said, "Oh no, only the best for my kid." The air had a venom in it, a hum like a live wire snapping electricity. "Make sure you pour it right. No head on that beer, Maury."

Maury handed Jack the glass. "Thanks," Jack said. He turned to leave. That's when he saw his Uncle Lou holding the paper and it stopped him.

Lou shook it at him, smirking. "Nice story, Jackie. Front page stuff, eh?"

"Fancy glass, fancy job," said Uncle Frank. The four men were all looking at him, waiting for something. He remembered one summer, on Aunt Anita's farm, when his uncles had taken him up to the well, hoisted him up, and pretended they were going to drop him in. His Uncle Lou had held his arms, dangling his feet in the giant well, which smelled dark and dank, like a cold, cold metal. *Dance, Jackie, dance.*

"Pass it over here," said Jack's dad, taking the paper. He read from the story in a high voice. "Across the street, in an abandoned museum, sits the one last artifact from the good ol' days of Wilkes-Barre." He looked over at Jack. "You proud of this?"

Jack knew he should just leave. They just wanted to mock him, knock him down a peg or two, show him he didn't belong.

"You proud of this? This rag? This shit paper that shits on its employees? Proud of betraying everything I taught you?" His father's voice was raised and slurred—he'd probably been drinking for hours—and he winked a glassy eye at Jack. "This is what I think of this." He threw the paper on the ground behind him. Turned. Unzipped his pants. The warm piss trickled off Jack's newspaper and onto the cold concrete, leaving a dark trickle of wet zigzagging toward the keg.

***

The Treadway was packed when Jack showed up. It wasn't hard to see *The Times Leader* folks, though, all gathered around the giant circular booth next to the bar. The Treadway had become their bar of choice since the strike, far enough out of town that picketers didn't show up looking to pick fights with scabs. It was a typical hotel bar, with lots of wood paneling and velvet-covered bar stools, but the drink specials were decent and they sometimes brought in live music on the weekends. Jack was in the mood for something simple like a whiskey and coke, but the mixed drinks were terrible—the soda was always flat and syrupy and they crammed the small glasses with ice—so he asked for a scotch straight up.

"I can't drink that stuff," Sophie said when he squeezed into the booth. There were too many of them, so he was jammed up next to her, their knees knocking under the table. She had changed into a small green dress and black tights and had swiped some kind of glittery stuff on her eyelids that sparkled under the dim light. He could smell her perfume and the smoke from the cigarette she'd just finished.

"Me neither," he said. "I bought it so I'd sip it." He tried to go into details about the peat and stuff, but his uncles' words about being fancy and pretentious came back to him, and he quit talking. On the other side of him, Gufstaski kept jabbing his elbow into Jack's shoulder as he re-enacted a disastrous attempt to cover a field hockey game where angry parents decided to boo him instead of the losing team.

"I'm glad you came," Sophie said.

"Was it a surprise?" Jack asked, the scotch starting to calm him.

"It was," she said. "It's a good thing I didn't bet on it. I would've lost."

"Me too," he said.

"So what changed your mind? Your great-granny decide to turn in?"

"My dad pissed on the newspaper," Jack said, swigging the rest of his shot without really meaning to. "So I said screw this."

Her eyes got wide, but she didn't ask anything. He felt bad saying anything about it at all. The whole thing left a sour taste in him, and he regretted not leaving it behind like he'd told himself to in the car. That crazy laughter, right out of a horror movie, bouncing around those bare walls as Jack just turned and left like a scared child.

Pussy. That had been his dad's parting word for him.

"How are you?" he asked.

She shrugged. "You know. Too bored to even kill myself."

Sophie turned to talk with her friend Dotty, who was an investigative reporter for the paper. They were scanning the bar, talking about guys. Sophie was laughing, but she seemed sad. He recognized the loneliness—it was something he was good at.

He looked away from her and realized he was crammed in the middle of a group of people with no one to talk to. He lit a cigarette for something to do.

The guys across from him leaned forward to tell their loud stories, and Jack had a sudden view across the bar to the back doors. He caught sight of a guy standing near them, hands in his pockets, surveying the room. He was short and stocky—when had the Treadway gotten bouncers?—but then the guy turned and something about his profile seemed familiar. Jack knew him, but he couldn't place him. Then Shemanski sat up, laughing at something and blowing smoke into the air above, and Jack's view was blocked.

"The toads, that's what they are," Shemanski said. "Like little warty people, squatting in this filthy house." He was talking about a murder he was covering—and by covering, that meant listening mostly to radio reports about the case and working his few contacts, since it was too dangerous for him to show up at the courthouse. Jack was trying to rejoin the conversation, but he felt very far away.

"What?" he asked, trying to focus.

"The family. They're all nasty, curled into one another. I thought they were going to spit at someone. You might wonder how a son could kill his mother, but spend five minutes with these people and you get it."

"Family can be the most brutal to each other, man," Jones said. "Feuds. Not surprising."

"It's really not surprising," Jack said, thinking of his dad. That dark trail of piss on the cold concrete. "And you can't choose your family."

The booth broke up. Some of the guys went to play pool on the coin table. Sophie and Dotty had taken posts at the bar chatting up two guys in suits that looked like they worked at a waterbed store. Jack slid out to refill his drink. It took him a while to even get to the bar. He ordered another scotch and took it to the bathroom.

Jack was washing his hands when he saw the bouncer-looking guy behind him in the mirror. The guy looked like a bull, his shoulders rounded forward like he was about to pounce. He knew him, that was for sure, but he still couldn't figure out from where. One of the picketers? Jack felt uneasy, thought about his picture and the knife. About Dotty getting harassed while in line at the bank to cash her check. About the picketers blocking the entrance to the building with their umbrellas. And that eternal burning barrel outside, the flames licking the dark at night.

Jack turned, dried his hands. The guy was blocking the door, and it wasn't until Jack was almost on top of him that he took a small step to the side. Jack swore the guy jabbed his shoulder out at him as he passed. A warning? Or was Jack just being paranoid?

Back in the bar, he ran into Shemanski. "Hey man, we're heading out. Sophie's guy showed up with some bunny, and she's buggin' out. You drove though, right?"

Jack nodded, was about to ask him about the bull man, and then didn't.

Sophie was right behind Shemanski, staring at something. He followed her gaze to a couple sitting at the bar, and he recognized her boyfriend right away. The boyfriend leaned in, whispered in the woman's ear, and took a suck on his cigarette.

Sophie looked at Jack. She opened her mouth a little, forming an 'o,' but before she could say anything he reached out and grabbed her arm. "You ready to go?"

The rain had picked up again. Shemanski, Sophie, and Jack gathered under the little awning outside the bar to say goodnight.

"You all right to drive?" Shemanski was looking at him with crinkled eyebrows. "Too much of that shitty scotch?"

"I'm cool."

Shemanski turned to Sophie. "You need a ride?" She looked quickly at Jack and he wondered if he should offer to drive her home. If that's what she wanted. But before he could decide, Sophie nodded at Shemanski. "That would be great," and the moment passed.

"See you guys Monday." Jack walked quickly across the parking lot as their laughter bounced off the asphalt and got dimmer. He was almost to his car when a shadow flickered across the parking space in front of him. He had barely enough time to register movement behind a large hedge lining the lot when he felt something heavy shove into his side. He heard the grunt of the words "fucking scab" and twisted on instinct. Whoever had lunged at him lost their balance and fell forward onto the roof of a parked car. The guy had been swinging a stack of newspapers— the heavy thing Jack had felt—and the pile burst open from their plastic band and scattered across the parking lot. The man rolled over and Jack recognized his face from the bar, those bullish shoulders rounded to charge again.

"Who are you?" Jack yelled, but the guy came at him again, swinging a fist. Jack ducked again, but this time the guy grabbed him around the chest and they both skidded on the newspapers and fell into the hedge. Short, prickly branches cut into Jack's face and arms as he tried to regain his balance. He rolled out, fell into the parking lot. The rain made it hard to see but the man was down again and Jack took that moment to kick him hard in the stomach.

"What the fuck, man?" The guy gasped, curling into a ball.

"You tell me what the fuck," Jack said, kicking him again.

"You know how many jobs you're taking away from people?" he spat up at Jack. "I hope you all die."

A car's headlights cut across the dimness. Jack looked up but all he could see were the raindrops pounding down in the light. Then the car swung around and stopped and Shemanski got out, running toward him.

Shemanski pushed Jack away and grabbed the guy's arm, pulling him up. For a moment, it looked like Shemanski was going to help the guy out, but as soon as bull man steadied on his feet, Shemanski pulled back and punched the guy in the jaw. "Asshole," he yelled at him. Then he turned to Jack. "You all right?"

Then Sophie was out of the car as well, in his face, looking at his cheek. "You got cut, I think. Let me see."

Jack shook them off. He could feel the blood pounding in his neck. "I'm fine, it's fine." He backed up, caught his breath. "Really."

Jack gathered up as many of the newspapers he could and threw them in his car. He could see they were tomorrow's run, fresh off the press, with spray paint all over the front.

"Do you want me to go inside and call the cops?" Sophie asked Shemanski.

"No, Christ. Don't do that." Jack said.

"Burn in hell. I don't care what you do to me," the bull man on the ground growled. "Go ahead. You've already ruined enough lives anyway. Why not one more?"

"Shut up," Shemanski said, kicking at him.

Jack's head was pounding. He backed up, gasped for air. The rain had let up into a mist, and the road looked like a slick river of oil. He snatched up the rest of the papers, hurling them into his back seat.

"Jack, what are you doing? Jack?" Sophie put her hands on his arms, trying to get in front of him. "Please stop."

He shook his head. He walked past her and got into his car. Before he could start the ignition, Sophie had flung open the passenger door and slid inside. He was too tired to argue, so he just peeled away with a loud screech.

***

He was driving too fast, feeling impatient with every car he met on the highway.

Fight back, fight dirty, Jack's dad was fond of saying. When Jack was in the third grade and Thomas McCaskey was stealing his lunch, Jack's dad tried to teach him how to fight. *Keep your thumb outside your fist when you punch someone. Go for the balls or the eyes.* Jack remembered fantasizing about stabbing McCaskey in the eyes, but when McCaskey came up behind him at recess and pushed him, skidding his elbows into the concrete, Jack did nothing. For weeks after, as his cuts healed, McCaskey would find ways to corner Jack, holding him down and scraping off the scabs until they bled again.

He thought of his dad and his uncles again, those menacing laughs. He wanted to rip off their scabs, dig into their old scars. Show them how it felt.

"Where did he get all those papers anyway?"

He'd almost forgotten Sophie was there. "A rack? I don't know why they keep putting them out."

She shook her head. He could see her eyes were shiny, but he didn't know if she was crying or angry. "I just can't believe this. They're all monsters."

Monsters. His dad used to play a game with him when Jack was little—chasing him around his bedroom, hiding behind the door and popping out. "More monster, more monster," Jack would beg, and his father would turn from reading the newspaper and contort his face, curving his hands into claws and roaring, much to Jack's delight.

Of course, he didn't really remember any of this. It was a story his mom and dad liked to tell, one they all laughed at. There was another story, too, one they didn't tell, one Jack never told either—a different kind of monster, his dad, this time when Jack was older and didn't find it funny anymore. His father, waiting for him in the darkness of the porch to come home one night and jumping out to scare him. Leaving dead fish in his boots if Jack forgot to put them in the closet. Making Jack dig a three-foot hole in the middle of the backyard to bury the pack of cigarettes he'd found under his bed.

Even before he realized where he was going, Jack had turned onto River Street, toward the suburbs. He traveled through the neighborhood he'd grown up in, each house in varying degrees of wear and tear, nearly every street dotted with a tiny beer garden for the locals, one of which his father might be sitting in right then, feet tucked under the stool.

"Where are we going?" Sophie's voice came quietly out of the dark.

"Nowhere," he answered. His parents' house was dark like all the other houses on the block. As he thought, his father's car was gone. Jack pulled up right in front.

Fancy foreigners, think they know everything.

"I'll be right back," he said to Sophie.

"What are you doing?" she asked as he opened the back door and pulled out wads of newspapers, but the rain drove out anything else she said.

He thought the wind might make his task more difficult, but as he lined his father's yard with the newspaper pages, the rain took care of it. He was making a sort of patchwork quilt, piece by piece, across the front lawn. He imagined his father waking up the next morning to soggy pieces of newspaper caking the entire yard, and how that would feel, how that was like one giant pissing on something you care about. After a while, he became aware of Sophie behind him, and he tried to ignore her, not wanting her to try to talk him out of it. He knew how he must look. But then he turned and saw she had some stacks of her own, that she was helping him. "You'll be soaked through at this rate," she yelled over the rain. "I thought you could use some help."

He didn't know how long it took. After a while it became a kind of game, he and Sophie working fast, even laughing as they backed into each other trying to cover all angles of the yard. Toward the end, the newspapers were beginning to dwindle, so they didn't cover every inch of it, but almost. In the dark, the dogwood tree in the middle of the lawn looked like it was growing through a lumpy, gray sand trap, the pulp from the wet pages disintegrating.

Back in the car, Sophie shook out her wet hair, spraying the windows. She shivered, turning the car's heating vents toward her. "And I thought I was nuts," she said, which made Jack laugh.

"It's my dad," he said. "It's a long story."

"Yeah. Pissing. Right on."

He couldn't tell if she was chiding him, and he felt a rush of guilt. "It's just, I don't know how to explain it."

"Don't worry, Jack," she said, leaning in. "I get it. Now, can we go somewhere dry?"

***

She didn't want to go home. Neither did he, but it was either that or drive around all night in the rain. His place was damp again, and he switched on the heater and turned on the lights.

"Sorry about this. Wasn't expecting company," he said, picking up an abandoned plate of egg sandwich from the night before.

She laughed. "Do you actually *live* here, Jack?"

"It's only been a month. Give me a break."

"I'm just kidding." She collapsed on his couch, hugging her knees to her chest.

"Do you want a sweater or something?"

She looked slightly dazed. "How about a shower? Do you mind?"

When she was in the bathroom, he changed into a dry shirt and went into the kitchen to pop an aspirin. His head was pounding. It felt like years since he'd been at the party talking to his mother and aunt. His hands were stained with newspaper ink, and though he washed them with dish soap, they still looked purple.

Something was bothering him about it all. The glee he'd felt back there on the lawn, getting even, was fading and now, instead of his dad, he kept seeing his mom waking up in the morning and looking outside to find what he'd done. Casualties of war, his uncles would probably say.

And here was Sophie in his apartment, in his shower. What did that mean? He didn't want it to be complicated. He was tired of complicated. All he wanted to do was nuzzle his face in her hair and lie down on the couch with her, a warm body. He wanted to sleep for a very long time.

She came out of the bathroom then, wrapped in his bathrobe and combing out her hair. She grinned at him. "My word, I could use a drink after all that. Got anything good?"

Jack didn't feel like drinking anymore, but he poured them both scotches and sat across from her. Sophie took a sip, closing her eyes and leaning back. Her neck looked very white. "God that felt good."

"The shower?"

She giggled. "No, silly. I mean, yes, that, too." She wiggled her toes into the space between the cushions. "After all the shit these jerks put us through...." She didn't finish her thought.

"I don't know. I feel like I've been hit by a cement mixer."

"Oh, you poor thing." She got up and settled down next to Jack, rested her glass on his knee, and smiled up at him. "I'm sorry. I didn't even ask how you were." She gently touched his face, pressed hers close to his. "Are you still bleeding?"

His soap smelled good on her, and the warmth of her skin made him even more tired. "I'll live."

"Fuck that guy."

"Yeah, fuck him," Jack said, grinning.

"I hope Shemanski killed him." She took a sip and held her glass up high. "Fuck my boyfriend, too."

Jack nodded, but didn't say anything.

"That girl he was with—did you see her? Wonder how much he paid her, anyway. God, I hate him." She tipped back the rest of her glass, fired up now, drinking too fast.

"I never liked him myself."

She smirked, got up, and poured herself another scotch. "Of course you didn't." She kneeled next to the television. "You mind?" she asked, and then flicked it on, turning to the late show. She settled back down next to Jack and lay her head down in his lap.

Jack hesitated, put his hand on her shoulder. She burrowed closer, murmuring, then turned up to look at him. "Fuck your dad, worst of all."

"Whoa," Jack said. "Worst of all?"

"Yeah, worst of all. What kind of dad does that to his own son? And after all you've done? All you've accomplished? He should be *proud* of you." Her words were clipped. "Worst of all."

"I don't know about that."

"Well, I do. He should be bragging to people about you, not pissing on you. Fuck him." She'd turned back to the TV, her voice quieter but still angry. "I wouldn't be surprised if we found out he sent that guy to the bar tonight."

"My dad wouldn't do that."

"You never know what people will do, Jack." She yawned. They sat in silence for a long time while on the television some comedian cracked jokes about things that Jack didn't find very funny. After awhile, Jack looked down and saw Sophie had fallen asleep, the light from the TV flickering dark shadows across her face.

He shifted out from under her. It hadn't been that comfortable anyway. During the next commercial, he got up from the couch. Sophie stirred, looked up at him, and smiled. "Where are you going?"

"I'll be right back," he whispered.

"Soon," she murmured and turned on her side. He wondered what she would think when she heard his front door close. If she heard it at all.

***

When Jack got to his parents' house, the papers were thoroughly wet, some already dissolving into something else. Jack started from the beginning, picking up the pages as best he could, shoving them into a plastic bag from his car. Jack sneezed and felt a tired ache run through his body. He was coming down with something, all the damn rain and dampness. He imagined what he must look like for any of the neighbors who happened to glance out their windows to see him, all bent over and tired, coughing, out of breath. Cold. The same way he'd imagined his dad raking it all up tomorrow morning.

What Jack could never tell his dad, even now: What it is, is: when the dirty deed is done, you still have to look at yourself in the mirror.

When Jack was done cleaning up, he would get back in his car and stop at the Dunkin' Donuts for some hot coffee. He'd go home and take a hot shower himself. He would sit with Sophie on the couch most of the night, if she was still there when he got back, and they would not sleep together. He might regret that some day when he was an old man with a raspy cough. He might regret a lot of things. But as he bent over, picking up the pulpy mess of the newspapers on his dad's thirty-year-old front lawn, he knew this would not be one of them.

Every Now and Then

David reinstates pizza and movie night, and he even volunteers to run down to the shopping center to pick it all up. "Do you want mushrooms?" He squeezes my side, all playful, none of the darkness flickering in the corners of his eyes. "I'll get a Disney movie for Seely."

"If you can tear her away from *Cinderella*," I say. It is playing for about the two hundredth time since we bought it a few months ago.

"And maybe another movie for us later," he says, fishing through his wallet for the card. "A thriller? You like those serial killer movies, right?"

***

Seely likes to run to the edge of the sand and watch the water come in, squealing and doubling back when the waves send shoots of spray she isn't expecting. She's three, her first time seeing the ocean. I am surprised she isn't afraid.

She gets sick of the surf and comes back to me, falling asleep curled up in the curve of my belly. David is helping one of the other kids on the beach build some kind of sand fortress with plastic molds. The air smells good, and the sand is warm in my hands. In a bit, we will pack up to shower off and head to the crab shack across the street for dinner. I love the business of eating hard shells—the hammering, the digging, working for your meat.

The squeal comes across the wind, a high cry of a boy in distress. He runs across the sand back toward his parents. David is following, holding his hands out from his side like he has something on them he needs to wash off.

The boy buries his head in his mother's shoulder. I get up, careful not to wake Seely. The wind turns sharp, snaps, as the sun hides behind a cloud.

***

I check out the window again. The air trembles just over our driveway where the heat bounces off the asphalt, hovering like a warning. The mailbox sits at the end of the drive, empty ever since the mail carrier Benita, fiddling with the crucifix around her neck, told me she was going to stop delivering to our house.

It wasn't surprising. She'd reported the Spencers for the slippery cherry blossoms on their sidewalk. And told Mr. Cratchet she didn't approve of his *Playboy* subscription.

"I just don't think it's right," she said to me. "It's been three times now. I've warned him. And with the school bus stopping right here on this street."

"What are you talking about?"

She shook her head, thrust the mail at me. "Maybe you should ask your husband."

***

"Is everything okay?" I look at David. His red swimsuit has flecks of sand on it, and I can see a line around his stomach where he's been sunburned.

The boy is babbling, his voice muffled by his mother's arm. "Castle... hurt." Then, "touched my ding ding."

"What did you do?" the father asks David sharply. The mother stands slightly away from all of us, shushing the boy. She throws me a dirty look, and I feel myself getting angry.

***

So I did ask him. That night while we were making dinner I said to David, "What did you do to Benita? She's freaking out."

"Oh no, now what?" David was cutting a tomato and I couldn't see his face. I told him about the conversation. It took him awhile to answer, just a little too long, and I began to feel my shoulders prick. Then he laughed. "Oh god. It's probably that one time I was walking past the front window in my boxers. You know what a prude she is. No wonder why she won't look at me anymore." He touched my arm, laughed again. "Don't worry. I'll talk to her. It's just a misunderstanding."

***

"Nothing, Jesus. Nothing. I...we were just playing in the sand and I reached over for one of the shovels and he jumped up like he was on fire." David looks more distressed than I've ever seen him.

The father shakes his head. He looks at me, confused, uncertain. His Hawaiian shirt flaps in the breeze like a flag. He looks at his wife and kid, then back at us, his face both defensive and embarrassed. "Nathan's been...well, he's been oversensitive lately, and...well."

"I'm really sorry, sir," David says. "I don't know what just happened."

"Paul," his wife says. An order. She says to us, "Just stay away from him." Then she walks off, and the husband follows, leaving behind their blanket and other things. It bothers me that they are abandoning their stuff.

***

Cinderella has found true love with her prince, and now Seely is hungry. "Where's Daddy?" she asks me, her chin on the kitchen table, looking bored.

"I think Daddy got tied up with something, Sweetie. I'm sure he'll call soon."

"But he was supposed to come back with pizza," she says.

"I know. I'm betting he's getting you a special surprise," I say.

"What kind of surprise?" she asks, picking up her head.

"One for princesses. One for very beautiful, special princesses." I pick her up, put her on my lap, and run my fingers through her hair. The strands are thicker, plentiful near the roots, but the ends thin out, trail off into pale blond wisps past her shoulders. I press my face to her head and breathe in her smell. I don't realize how tight I'm hugging her until Seely wiggles out of my grasp and slides to the floor.

"Mommy, you're weird. I'm going to watch for Daddy," she says, skipping out of the kitchen in her yellow socks.

It's no good to check the clock again. It's no good to call—David's cell sits on the coffee table.

Twenty minutes later I pull a pizza out of the freezer and turn on the oven.

***

We walk the boardwalk. Seely wants an endless stream of quarters for candy, soda, rides on mechanical animals. She wants to press her own penny to say "Ocean City Forever." She wants popcorn and neon colored t-shirts.

At the end of the night, she and David go in one final store while I stay outside, resting my feet on a bench. Next to me, a family of four is arguing. The two boys want to head in the direction of the Ferris Wheel, and the parents want food. "No, damn it," the father says finally. "We're a family. We stick together."

A young teenage boy with one of those handheld cart trolleys rolls by me and points. "Lovely lady all alone!" he says in a thick Italian accent. "You come. I give you ride. Wherever you want to go."

The family looks over. The father cracks a smile. I shake my head, embarrassed. "No, no. I'm waiting for my husband," I say. "He'll be here any minute."

***

At about 10:00 p.m., when I am about to lose it, the phone rings. I hear the deep, stern male voice on the other end and my heart sinks. "Is this Mrs. Rivers?"

The officer's voice washes over me. I catch every fourth or fifth word. "Your husband…pinball…parking lot…two boys…circling…" At first they thought it was a joke, a misunderstanding. Then they saw.

***

And then I see Seely, skipping towards me, her little body shaking with excitement. "Daddy bought me a pet!" she says, and then I see David behind her, carrying a small plastic cage with an orange lid.

"Hermit crab," he says, shrugging. "They were five bucks. She liked its shell."

"The shell is his house, Mommy. It's where he lives. Daddy says he carries it around with him all the time, so he always has a place to stay."

I give David a look, but really it doesn't matter. We're all happy. She names him Pepper Pants.

***

I grab a pink duffle bag from Seely's closet and start shoving things into it, my hands steady with purpose. Seely mumbles something and tries to roll over. I let her go, zipping up the bag and heading to my bedroom. I change my shirt, put on fresh deodorant. I brush on powder like I'm preparing for a date.

"Mommy, what's going on?"

I jump, turn. Seely's standing there, her eyes squinting in the bright bathroom. "Jesus, you scared me sweetheart."

"Why are my clothes on the floor?"

"We are going on an adventure." I try to sound bright, positive, but it falls flat.

"Where's Daddy?"

"He can't come with us right now," I say, kneeling down beside her.

Seely's face scrunches up. I can see the tears already pooling. "I don't want to go without Daddy."

"He'll see you later, honey. He just can't come now."

"No. I don't want to go anywhere without him." She starts wailing now, the kind of cry I haven't heard since she was an infant. I pick her up, and she kicks, finding my stomach, and I nearly drop her. The pain comes fast, spreading through my gut. I bite my lip not to scream. I am amazed at how badly I want to slap her, pull her hair back, anything to get her to shut up.

***

When we come back from the beach, the cage is empty. We search the room—under the bed, in the toilet, comb the dirty, busy-patterned carpet.

"Hermit crabs don't move fast," David says. "They don't jump. They don't do any damn thing. Where could it have gone?"

Seely is upset. She cries. She wants us to keep looking, even after an hour. She wants us to call the hotel manager to see if he's seen him.

"We can go get another one," I tell her. "Tomorrow morning. You can pick him out."

"I want Pepper Pants," she says. David puts his sandals on.

"I'll go give the hotel guy a description," he says. He comes back twenty minutes later with a paper bag tucked under his shirt. Five minutes later we find Pepper Pants in the shower. It is a miracle.

***

I tell Julie next door there's a small emergency and she agrees to come over. Her hair is damp and she looks flushed, like she just got out of the shower. "Is everything okay?"

"Yes, yes, it's fine," I say. "David just got into a car accident. Really minor, but they're telling him not to drive so I've got to go get him."

She clucks. "Oh, David. He's always got such bad luck, doesn't he?"

***

Later that night, after we put Seely to sleep, it is a joke between us. David's eyes glisten charmingly as he pulls me close. We lay in the dark on the king-size bed in the hotel laughing about all of it. "Hey Pepper Pants, I'm going to touch *your* ding ding," I tell him, my hand fumbling under the covers.

Death Wish

Sandra's manager sent people home early because of the murder. He told everyone that the in-house therapist was available for counseling sessions, but Sandra left at noon. She sat in her car in the parking lot of her apartment building, not really wanting to go inside. A young woman with short red hair walked a small beagle past Sandra's car. The woman smiled at her, her hand full of mail. The dog was sniffing snow. It seemed so ordinary, so disrespectful.

It was hot in her apartment and the air smelled of meat and something else, maybe mold. Amy was playing Christian rock music loudly, and as Sandra walked past the kitchen, she turned around, spatula to her mouth.

"Do you want some meatloaf?" Amy held out the pan like a prize, a brownish lump inside.

"No thanks." Sandra went to her room and closed the door. Amy was quiet and mousy, her thinning hair always greasy and tangled. She was thirty-two-years old and looked like she was fifty. Sandra had met her through craigslist when she moved to town, and the rent was cheap so she'd said what the hell. Amy was nice enough, but the religious thing kind of got to Sandra. Through the walls Sandra could hear little children singing on Amy's stereo, "Call me if you need me, I'll be doing work for the Lord." It reminded her of a cult, of little kids with chains around their feet digging in unison.

Sandra got undressed and turned the shower water as hot as she could stand it, letting the water crash into her hair and down to her feet. She kept thinking of Debbie, who had been at work on Friday, doing her job as usual, and now was just a grainy picture in the newspaper, a covered body being carried away by officials, a right arm hanging limply off a stretcher. They hadn't been friends, had only talked a few times, exchanged office jokes and occasionally took messages for each other, but now that Debbie was dead, it seemed that Sandra could only think of nice things about her. Debbie had sat in the cubicle right across from Sandra and had shared her portable heater. She bought Sandra a potted plant for Christmas last year. She had a nice smile and she always ordered candy from the PTA moms in the office.

They both had boyfriends named Dave, and when Debbie's Dave came to pick her up for lunch sometimes, Debbie would point to the photo of Sandra's Dave on her desk and joke about how their boyfriends even looked alike. They were the Doublemint Daves, like the twins on that silly gum commercial. Two Daves, both tall with brown hair and glasses. Debbie's Dave was funnier than Sandra's Dave, who usually only joked out of sullenness. Debbie's Dave was funny and sweet. He brought Debbie things, fast food kid's meal toys and candy that cluttered her desk. Debbie's Dave had once told her she looked like Sandra Bullock. "Why, that's her first name!" Debbie had said, and Sandra had blushed.

"See, there you go. It was meant to be." Debbie's Dave had laughed and winked at Sandra, pulling his hand through his already-ruffled hair.

Sandra rinsed the conditioner from her hair and stepped out, wrapping a robe around herself. In the kitchen, she got a glass of ice water and drank it quickly. Amy stood near the front door watching Sandra, hands shoved in the pockets of the hunting coat that was too big for her. She never carried a purse.

"Why are you home so early?" she asked.

Sandra sat down at the kitchen table and began combing through the knots in her hair, spraying water across the table and the newspaper.

"Someone died," Sandra said, staring straight at Amy.

"Oh." Amy stepped back awkwardly, pressing against the door. "I'm sorry."

"It wasn't really anyone I knew," she said so that her roommate would leave. Amy nodded and turned, closed the door behind her without locking it. When she was gone, Sandra threw the deadbolt, pressing her cheek against the cold door. She could hear the wind whistling through the stairwell of the apartment complex like a spirit.

***

Her Dave called at work the next day to ask if she wanted to see a hockey game. "I got extra tickets from work for this Friday. Isn't that great?" He got extremely excited over free stuff. He was disturbingly frugal, driving all around to find the best gas prices and stacking neatly clipped coupons, divided into categories, on the kitchen counter. She knew she would have to smuggle bags of candy in her purse.

"I've never been to a hockey game before," she told him.

"Well, then all the more reason to be excited. It's a great game. The fights are the best part."

Dave lived on the other side of town, alone, so they often spent time there. She enjoyed his apartment because it was always so warm. "You have good heat," she told him the first time she spent the night, a few months after they started dating. They'd met through an online dating service and she'd been relieved at how easy he was to talk to. She needed someone. It was hard being alone in a new city.

Sandra liked to take naps in Dave's bed, but didn't like it when he tried to cuddle up next to her for a kiss. Once the first kiss happened, he'd immediately start taking off her shirt. It was like clockwork—she could time it. It disgusted her, really, and one time when she'd pulled away and asked him, "Haven't you heard of foreplay?" he'd looked at her blankly and nipped at her ear.

This was the problem, she knew. She wanted Dave for the companionship. When she spent time with him she wanted to watch a movie or put a puzzle together—not fuck him silly. He was nice, if a bit immature, and when he looked at her with those glazed-over, desiring eyes, she didn't know whether to giggle or gag.

Without Dave, there was only Amy and her coworker Beth, who she went out with occasionally but didn't feel close to. Once they went to a small, country line dancing bar where everyone threw peanut shells on the floor. Beth wore a tight, button-down shirt with fringe, a miniskirt, and big boots, and yee-hawed to every song. No, Dave was better than being lonely. He was a stick in a big puddle of mud.

***

The gossip was in full swing at work. Sandra couldn't walk down the halls without seeing people in huddles, whispering. At lunch, Beth told Sandra they'd arrested Debbie's Dave. "I heard they found him in her house, that they took him out in handcuffs," Beth said. "He was going through her stuff. Pictures and things. I think he was trying to cover his tracks."

"I don't really believe that. I don't think it was someone she knew." Sandra paused. She stabbed at her salad and remembered Debbie's Dave's laugh. "He was such a nice guy."

"They might come in to investigate her cube—look at files on her computer. They do that, you know. They have all these ways of figuring out stuff."

Sandra poured over the articles in the paper and examined the pictures of him as though they held a clue to what really happened. The Doublemint Dave—a murderer? She'd have known. She would have been able to see it in his eyes.

During the day, Sandra would look up and stare at the desk where Debbie used to work. The management had taken all her stuff away and cleaned it off. It was like they wanted to wash away the terribleness, sweep it under the plastic mat Debbie wheeled her computer chair on to keep the carpet from getting ruined. Only one trace of her remained—a small, circular green sticker she'd stuck in the corner of her computer monitor that read, "Love Me, I'm a Vegetarian!" the "i" dotted with a little red tomato. Sandra picked at it with her fingernail, but it was too sticky to come off without ripping so she left it there.

***

As expected, Dave wanted to eat dinner before the hockey game. "Eight bucks for a hotdog? Don't think so. Want some leftover steak?" He pulled out a dinner plate, covered tightly with sunken-in plastic wrap, and placed it in the microwave.

"I told you I'm not eating meat anymore," she reminded him with a glare.

"Oh, that's right," he said. "That's this week's decision."

"What do you mean, this week's decision?" She backed away from him and hit her head on the knob of one of his cabinet drawers.

"Ah, come here." Dave hugged her, trapping her arms. He rubbed her head and kissed her hairline. "Do you need ice? I think you'll live."

"You're making fun of me."

"Oh, come on."

"I hate it when you patronize me."

He shook his head. "You know I like you too much for that."

"Yeah, Debbie's Dave used to say that to her and look what happened."

He snorted. She picked the lumps of fat from his meat off the countertop and tossed them in the sink in disgust, flipping on the garbage disposal. It made a dull humming noise, like a sick bird, and she could smell metal burning.

"Oh, it's broken," Dave said over his shoulder.

She peered down the drain. "Why don't you fix it?"

"I don't know how," he said, licking his fingers.

"Wasn't there a movie where this guy killed his girlfriend, chopped up her body, and fed it to the garbage disposal?" She wanted to irritate him. Had Debbie and her Dave been standing in the kitchen like this? Debbie, fixing a drink, while Dave came up behind her with a kitchen knife? Was it jealousy? Did he think she was sleeping with another man? Sandra remembered Debbie telling her something once about him not liking when she went out with her friends.

"I think there was the one where he killed her, burned her body in the industrial sized oven, and then vacuumed up her ashes," Dave said, laughing. He grinned and she felt like flicking his nose, imagining his expression. She wished that they fought, screamed at each other, threw plates or something, anything to chip away at the level landscape of sameness. He leaned over the table and punched her shoulder softly. "Come on, Sandy. What's going on with you? Are you still upset about that girl at work?"

***

Their seats for the game were two rows from the top. They had to shuffle past two people already seated in the aisle. Sandra and Dave had seats three and four, but Dave shifted over two so that they left a few seats between them and the other couple.

"But what if these people come?" she asked.

"Then we'll move," he said.

The national anthem played and the game began. Dave tried to explain it all to her, but she just saw a bunch of men skating around. It was too fast to keep up, and she wasn't sure where she was supposed to look. A few minutes into the game, a couple came up to their row, held up their tickets, and looked at Sandra.

"We have seats five and six," the woman told Sandra coldly, as people around them shuffled in their seats to see the game.

"That's fine," Sandra said weakly, glaring at Dave. The two of them shifted over.

Sandra sat down glumly next to Dave, who was completely oblivious. "Get off yer knees, ref, and stop blowing the game!"

Sandra felt her cheeks get hot. The couple that had just arrived were quiet and well-dressed, probably coming straight from some important work meeting. And now she was sure they did not like her, thanks to Dave.

When the team scored, Dave jumped up and pumped his fists. He started singing along to the fight song and clapping his hands in unison with the guy in front of him. The two of them slapped a high five, as if they personally had something to do with the goal. When the other team came back and scored two goals in a matter of seven minutes to pull ahead, Dave began cursing. "Stop playing like a bunch of pansies and make it entertaining for us!"

Their seats were so high up that if she stood to leave Sandra thought she might pitch forward and fall, banging limbs as she gained momentum. She studied Dave's profile, his slack chin, the hair behind his ear. His hands were clenched, his eyes focused on the action. It would be easy for him to kill her. He could do it with his bare hands. Snap her neck, like that.

The guy in front of them stood up suddenly, and then Dave did, and everyone tensed. Sandra watched as one of the players grabbed an opponent by the head. His helmet was off, his hair wild and sticky from sweat, and he punched the other guy in the stomach repeatedly. The crowd was cheering.

"Fuckin' A! Yeah! Yeah!" Dave yelled. The referee came to break up the fight, but not before the helmetless guy spit on his opponent's face. He skated into the penalty box and the crowd booed.

She turned to Dave to ask him if they could leave, but he grabbed some popcorn and winked at her. "Now we're ready for some hockey, right, babe?" He pumped his fist.

The woman next to her looked over, smiling tensely. "Your boyfriend's funny," she said. "He really gets into it, doesn't he?"

***

They went most of the way home in silence. Amy was awake, watching television in the dark, her glasses reflecting the late night dating show. She clutched her pillow, eating Doritos from the bag between her legs. They walked past her and into Sandra's room, shutting the door.

Dave threw himself on her bed, making the wall shake. "Come here, sweetheart."

She curled next to him and faced the wall. He snaked his arm around her and under her shirt. He would go for the nipple immediately—ah, yes, there it was. His breathing got heavy. She wiggled away.

"Dave, I…"

He kissed her, hard. She could taste the beer and the salt from the popcorn as his tongue explored her mouth. He pressed harder and slid on top of her, covering her body. He was tall, his weight smothered her, and she tried to push him off. But he grabbed her arms, pulling them above her head, and smiled at her. She thought she saw something cold behind his eyes. She felt her heart beating as she stared into his face, this man she didn't really know at all.

"Oh, baby," he moaned, nipping at her ear. It amazed her that two people could be in the same room and have completely different ideas about what was going on. She couldn't breathe and she struggled against him. He grabbed her arms tighter, held both of her wrists with his one hand, his other moving south, tugging on the button of her jeans. She thought about Debbie. She wondered if it was worse to be dead or completely alone, or if the two were even all that different.

"No," she said again, louder. She twisted, pulling her knee upwards into his crotch. He screeched and rolled over.

"Sandy, what the hell?" She pushed herself off the bed and stood up, breathing heavily. He looked at her, still doubled over, his eyes confused. "What the hell is wrong with you?"

"I said I didn't want to."

"Yeah. Painfully."

"I'm sorry. I guess I'm just still thinking about what happened at work." She couldn't look at him. "I think you should leave."

He reached for her and she recoiled. She saw him flinch. "I don't understand what just happened," he said, holding out his hands, palms up, like a peace offering.

He followed her out into the living room, where Amy still sat pinching her lower lip. Dave put his coat on. "I'll call you," he said tersely, and left, slamming the door.

Amy looked up from the show, a slight smile on her face. "Everything all right?"

***

Eventually they hired someone else to sit at Debbie's old desk—a blonde woman, tall and lean, who had a little maple leaf pin on her coat and always wore dark brown lipstick. Her name was Nelly and Sandra made sure to introduce herself the first day. Nelly was married with three children and her husband's name was Frank. She had pictures of her kids tacked on the walls of her cubicle, and she covered the "I'm a Vegetarian!" sticker with a laminated copy of the poem "Footprints."

At lunch, Beth and Sandra still obsessed over Debbie's murder trial. Beth remembered things she hadn't thought of before—how one time he told her he'd stolen a pack of cigarettes, how she thought she might have seen him once on *America's Most Wanted*. "Should I say something to the police? Do you think they'd want to know?"

Sandra watched Debbie's Dave on television while Amy cooked in the kitchen. If the reception was fuzzy, he looked almost exactly like her

Dave, only now with a beard. She used to dream about him sometimes, before Debbie had been killed. She used to think maybe she could take him away from Debbie and have him all to herself.

***

Sandra stopped calling her Dave and made excuses when he asked her to go out. Sometimes they ran into each other in the city, and she would feel a stab of guilt and have lunch with him. She spent the nights she would've been out with him watching Debbie's Dave's trial on television, sometimes even sharing a bowl of popcorn with Amy, who was convinced he was going to get the death penalty. Spring turned into summer. Her Dave put his profile back up on the dating site. Hockey season ended.

One night, several months after Debbie's Dave was convicted, Sandra came home from being out with Beth and couldn't sleep. She heard an ambulance siren and sat up to peer out of her window at the parking lot. The young woman with short red hair was walking her dog, headed for the wooded path that snaked behind the complex. She disappeared behind the trees alone. It was so late at night.

She began writing a letter on yellow legal paper. She wrote about the young woman and her dog, about fear, about how it was odd that something so small could seem so horrifying. She wrote about the way Beth danced with strangers in bars, her hips pressed forward, lips against their necks. She was writing to Debbie's Dave. She could picture him opening the letter in his cell, running his hand through his hair like she remembered. The thought was like biting into chalk. She told him about Amy, how she ordered chocolate milk in restaurants and sprayed Lysol on the phone after she used it. She told him about her Dave, how he had never seemed to understand what it was she was feeling, how their relationship would've been a long, sturdy rectangle with no bumps or grooves. She filled five pages with her handwriting, feeling reckless.

When she was finished, she folded the letter into thirds, sealed it in an envelope without re-reading it, and went online to find the address of the prison. She thought again of the young woman walking her dog as she put on her sneakers and robe and grabbed her keys off the dresser, feeling slightly crazy as she quietly closed the apartment door. She knew if she thought about it too long she would lose her nerve. The mailbox was at the end of the parking lot. The night was sticky, the cicadas loud in their unrelenting buzzing, and Sandra ran, her heart thumping, imagining she was going to be grabbed from behind at any point. The mailbox pulled open with a creak, and she fed it the letter. Racing back to the apartment, robe billowing behind her, Sandra wondered, briefly, elatedly, how she must look, and hoped there was someone watching her run.

Acknowledgments

This manuscript wouldn't exist without the help of some very lovely people. Thank you to all the editors of all the fine journals that first took a chance on some of these stories. Thanks to my MFA writing group and professors at George Mason University, who read a few of these stories in early draft and helped make them better. I especially want to note my professor and friend Alan Cheuse, who introduced me to some of my most favorite books and stories and encouraged my love for words. He is and will continue to be dearly missed. Cheers to Dotty Martin, who lived through *The Times Leader* newspaper strike and graciously shared her stories with me. A special shout-out to Laura Ellen Scott, Brandon Wicks, Katie Rawson, Isaac Boone Davis, Ann Laskowski, and Beth Posniak Fiencke for giving me invaluable comments on the manuscript and catching some silly mistakes. I also want to thank my family for all their support, especially my husband Art Taylor, whose writing advice, wisdom, and encouragement keeps me going every single day.

The following stories were previously published in slightly different versions in these publications:

"The Witness," *Santa Fe Writers Project Journal*, November 2010
"There's Someone Behind You," *So to Speak*, Winter/Spring 2009
"The Monitor," *Alfred Hitchcock's Mystery Magazine*, April 2014
"Happy and Humpy," *Lake Effect*, January 2013
"Half the Distance to the Goal Line," *Hot Metal Bridge*, December 2011
"The Oregon Trail," *The Hawaii Review*, Spring 2014
"Every Now and Then," *Amazing Graces: More Fiction by Washington Area Women*, January 2012
"Death Wish," *Phoebe*, Spring 2005

About the Author

Tara Laskowski is the author of *Modern Manners for Your Inner Demons*. She was awarded the Kathy Fish Fellowship from *SmokeLong Quarterly* in 2009, and won the grand prize for the 2010 Santa Fe Writers Project Literary Awards Series. Her fiction has been published in the Norton anthology *Flash Fiction International, Alfred Hitchcock's Mystery Magazine, Mid-American Review*, and numerous other journals, magazines, and anthologies. She has been the editor of *SmokeLong Quarterly* since 2010 and lives in Virginia with her husband, toddler, and two whiny cats.

www.taralaskowski.com

Also from Santa Fe Writers Project

The Poor Children *by April L. Ford*

Ford explores the eccentric, the perverse, the disenfranchised, and the darkly comic possibilities at play in us all.

"From the amazing first sentence of April L. Ford's debut collection, The Poor Children, *I was hooked. This is a rarity: a compellingly original voice and vision."*
— David Morrell,
New York Times *bestselling author*

Muscle Cars *by Stephen G. Eoannou*

A powerful journey through the humor, darkness, and neuroses of the modern American Everyman...

"Eoannou's debut collection is all—all—heart."
—Brett Lott, author of Jewel,
an Oprah Book Club Selection

About Santa Fe Writers Project

SFWP is an independent press founded in 1998 that embraces a mission of artistic preservation, recognizing exciting new authors, and bringing out of print work back to the shelves.

Find us on Facebook, Twitter @sfwp, and at www.sfwp.com

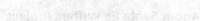